PULLED
FROM THE
RIVER

Rochester, New York does not exist.

PULLED FROM THE RIVER

JON CHOPAN

BLACK LAWRENCE PRESS

www.blacklawrencepress.com

Executive Editor: Diane Goettel
Cover Image: Greg Cunneyworth
Cover Design: Greg Cunneyworth
Book Design: Steven Seighman

ISBN: 978-1-936-87369-2

First edition: December 2011

Printed in the United States of America

10 9 8 7 6 5 4 3 2 1

CONTENTS

This book is for my mother, who is always here hidden away in the bright lights, for my father, Jeff, and Ralph.

"All this happened, more or less."
–Billy Pilgrim

None of them
Thought to write a book

About the flight
Across frozen lakes

Or the dead
Who look for us

During our lives.
They went on drinking tea

Without ambition—
Like men who remain

Where their houses once stood.

Stephan Kuusisto, *Helsinki* 1958

PULLED FROM THE RIVER

I

When I tell you this story, remember it may change: My father collected garbage that piled in our backyard and toward the sky. He knew the value of discarded things. "I found this one on my way home from work," he'd say. "This is one of the first microwaves ever made." You could find him rummaging through the trash or scavenging along the banks of the river where bottles floated to the shore.

II

We were boys growing up along the Genesee River with backpacks full of stuff, trophies taken along the way. Some days we'd walk along the railroad tracks behind the zoo and collect rocks and Indian arrowheads. We'd chase one another, throwing moss and mud - and when the winter hit, snow. I always liked to think we were explorers or soldiers. We went to the woods because we felt safe there. Or, we went because we didn't.

III

I heard the river talking to me sometimes. *Do not come near me,* it said. Or sometimes it said, *do.* There are so many secrets hidden in the water. As a child I was afraid of the river. I swam in it only once, in the spring when the water was still cold and the current had just begun to pick up. I was no swimmer, but I thought I could make it from one bank to the other. I only made it halfway and was lucky to turn around and come back. The current dragged me down river and I returned to my friends very wet.

IV

I was wrong. There was a second time, when I was fishing with my father and he threw me in. It was the summer, and I had on a life vest and he told me to just put my feet down. "Stop flailing around and stand up," he said. I remember the way the floor of the river felt: the muddy surface oozing between my toes, how cold it was despite the warmth of the water and the summer sun.

V

Hidden beneath the surface: carp, walleye, catfish, bottles of Pepsi and Coke and Genny beer, and bodies, of course. The body of Ruben's mother. The body of my friend Pony who jumped from the walking bridge. The bodies of less fortunate swimmers.

VI

We believed in monsters. The real kind. Frankenstein and Dracula and ghosts too.

VII

Let's say I made everything else up. My father never collected things; I never swam the river; and they never found Pony's body, his long, sand-filled hair stinking of the Genesee. All I am is the son of a janitor, a man who wears clothes with holes in them, who tells stories, who comes from a place that knows only stories and the retelling of them. He wears old military issue glasses; he drinks coffee by the pot. Occasionally he even tries to get our mother, his ex-wife, to go out to dinner with him. My father was a solider and he knows that a good story grows with each telling. Tells us that stories should be told over a beer on a hot summer day, over fishing, while walking on railroad tracks.

VIII

Walking on the tracks you'd hear someone say: "How do you know?" Or, "It didn't happen like that." We talk like we were all there when they pulled Pony's body from the water, but we weren't.

IX

Standing out on the bridge late at night, we drank and threw things in, listening for the sound of the river calling back. We imagined how Pony jumped from that bridge or what it was like under the water. I could see his dark green eyes blinking and opening again. I could make out his pale, freckled skin, before he disappeared into the water. "Seems like it would have been a rush." We sit, all of us imagining it, the wind through our hair, the water and the things in it, the sound of traffic on the memorial bridge overhead, the current drawing him toward the bottom. "Pony," we called him, because he was the runt among us. This is the only way to craft a story that will bring him back.

X

Maybe this is really about my father, about the syrup factory he comes to live in years after he throws me in the river. Or, maybe this is about the high rise he lives in after that. They both border the river; they are both pieces of a memory that swirls around it.

XI

Maybe it was a serial killer who inspired our belief and not the movies. Maybe it wasn't Pony's body at all but the body of Ruben's mother, her long black hair soaked in river water and reflecting the flashes from the crime scene cameras. Do you remember how that killer went after women? Do you remember how young we were and how Ruben heard it in the hallways and got made fun of? Maybe Ruben knew, years before, while he was being breastfed or walking home from school that it was coming. Maybe he was even there the night that man killed her. The abandoned tugboat we grew up on passed through town that night destined to become our hideout, our place for stashing memories. I remember his mother's tanned skin, and the way she smelled, and how we'd always say to Ruben, "Your mom is so hot!" But do you remember Ruben? How he asked that girl who came to visit our class why she wore a hat even though the teacher told us not to because she had cancer and had lost her hair to treatments? Do you remember how the teacher nervously explained that Ruben had just lost his mother, murdered, how he was a wild kid, and how he couldn't control himself? On the playground he sat alone or chased girls or never got picked for dodge ball.

XII

All those memories are at the bottom of the river where that tugboat finally sank the summer I turned 21 or 26 or maybe it didn't sink,

but is going down right now. My father and I ran into Ruben
years after that day in grade school. He looked just like the boy
I remembered sitting alone, his curly black hair like his mothers,
and his hazel eyes. I thought I'd buried that memory. But there
it was, that snapshot, standing at a cash register waiting for me to
checkout.

XIII

You remember it your way and I'll remember it mine.

XIV

If I drag it up from the bottom of the river, if I dig deep into that
muddy floor and pull it up, even if I get most of it wrong, is it mine
to tell? Pony is dead and Ruben is gone, and my father's collection
has dwindled down to the few things he could fit into his minivan.
All I have are scraps from the pile.

XV

Every passion borders on chaos, that of the collector on the chaos of memory.
A) How cold that water was. B) The smell of it, the river, when
you're passing over with the car windows open. C) What we've
thrown into it that will never come up and what we've seen sink to
the bottom.

XVI

I am sitting at my father's apartment having coffee. He wants me to
tell him a story, one that is not about him. "Perhaps it can be about
monsters or the river," he says. "Start with 'Once upon a time' and
let it go from there. One of the ones you told me when you were a
kid or liked me to tell you." I tell him that I don't know where to

start. All I have are pieces. I've given up on monsters and maybe even on story. "Do you want the truth or fiction?" I ask. And he says not to worry about story, not to worry about fact or fiction. "Just give me the pieces," he says. "I'll find the story and that will be truth enough."

THIS FORM OF GRIEVING

My father moved into the old syrup factory on East Main Street with a futon and his photography equipment. My mother told him to leave and never come back. He took pictures of the train yard behind his building. He smoked cigarettes in his 12' by 10' room, looking out at the trains coming and going. He wrote me letters on the back of his photographs. His move was good for us, both him and me. It was the first time, through his photos, that we'd really talked.

"Thoreau bragged that Concord could show him nearly everything worth seeing in the world or nature," my father wrote. "He did not need to read Dr. Kane's 'Artic Voyages' for phenomena that he could observe at home." This was written on the back of a photo of the directory at the syrup factory listing residence and businesses residing there. My father, living on the second floor in room 214, was above "Always Fresh Pasta," and below "The Pool Players Association." This card arrived on a Friday and was the first he sent. I think he meant it to explain his leaving.

His photos were mostly of odd things like the directory. Street signs, parking lots, homeless people living at underpasses.

He had old equipment, things he'd pulled from other people's garbage or bought after he'd come home from the Vietnam War. But, that thirty-year-old equipment, those recycled parts, were antiques, and his photos were shot, mostly, with disposable cameras, developed at Wal-Marts and Kmarts around Rochester.

My father started going to black churches, the Rochester City Youth Boxing competitions, obscure punk shows at a place called *The Laundromat*. By night he is a janitor at a home for the elderly and during the day he is a photographer, except for his nights off when he goes to bars and to soup kitchens and to other places like that where he can take photos. He sneaks naps at work and only occasionally gets caught.

My brother, Jeff, and I go with him to bars and strip clubs. We get drunk and he drinks Labatt Nordic, a non-alcoholic beer, because he drives us in his '94 Dodge Caravan, which has a makeshift bed in the back where he can sleep. We do not join him on his other photo expeditions and he does not ask us to. A photographer needs to concentrate on his subjects, needs to avoid distractions.

When we are with our father we are his subjects and his sons. At The Klassy Cat, where women dance topless and he cannot bring his camera, he says to us, "You know, you can become addicted to women just like anything." Later Jeff turns to me, a dancer in his lap and a bottle of beer in his hand. He grins. "It's fantastic!"

This is how we spend time with our father, both here and in his letters, and I feel, even later at a bar when he is taking photos of us, that he does it all because of a sense of loss or fear of it. A boy was killed the night before our trip to the Klassy Cat. He was shot a street over and his killers took his shoes. He went to the same high school as us. It was like my father imagined it was one of us.

There were posters all over telephone poles with that boy's name, with pictures of him. They were looking for his killers. They were offering a reward for information leading to arrests. And I could see, by the way he talked that night, by the pictures he was taking, that those killers being on the loose scared my father.

A photographer must be unmovable. He must be able to shoot any picture at any moment no matter the gore or inhumanity. The photographer knows that his prints are a way of capturing the world, a way of saving it, if only for a second, so that others cannot deny or turn away.

I leaf through my father's photos when I haven't seen or heard from him for days or weeks. This is my way of communicating with him. I send letters to him as well. I don't write on photographs, but occasionally I send him old ones he took when we were kids and dressed us up with fake noses and mustaches and glasses. Photography has been his way of loving us. You can see him in these photos, the way he has studied the reflections, the lighting he has meticulously worked on, and though he does not appear in any they always contain him.

Jeff and I look for our father when we go out. He can be anywhere. Men standing on a corner. Car accidents. He can be taking pictures of anything. There is always something in the city that requires his attention.

It's a way of understanding the world, the camera. Always, our father's way of understanding it. His father before him worked on the railroad, and on the back of one of his photos (a train passing by the syrup factory) he writes: "My father worked for 25 years or so for the railroad. Baltimore and Ohio. B & O. Guess my interest in them stems from this." Sometimes when I look close I am sure I see ghosts in his photographs. Some believe a camera is the only thing that can capture them.

When we do not see our father we often run into his friends. They, like us, are not photographers but people from his photographs.

Visits go like this: my father offers us food he's purchased at the Farmer's Market. 40 tomatoes for a dollar. Three bushels of bananas for two. Radishes, apples, peppers. His room looks like the produce section at the grocery store. He cuts up vegetables, pours salt on them, and we eat while we flip through new photographs or as he tells us where he is thinking of shooting that night. We drink beer, which is what we've brought as a "visiting gift." My father bums cigarettes from my brother. We leave when he is ready to go out.

He doesn't have a phone so visits are "At your own risk." And if he isn't there and his neighbor is, the neighbor is likely to bother us for change or if we've come with beer to bother us for one of them. If my father is there the door will be open, unless he is asleep, which he never is. If you miss him you leave a note with the next time you plan on coming by. Otherwise just try back later.

If he's not in the apartment we check the train yard or walk the half mile down to the river where he might be shooting photos or talking with friends or just relaxing and having a beer or fishing. All his neighbors and people around the area know him and have come to know us.

He'd always, for some reason, have corn boiling in a hot pot. He'd say that the corn from the market was the best you could get anywhere. He'd make four or five ears at a time as if he were expecting us or some other company. I'd ask him about spots he'd been shooting lately and he'd show me photos but never talk about them, what he did there other than shooting photos—if anything. A good photographer has secrets. A good photographer always falls just a little in love with his subjects.

———

One night Jeff and I drove my buddy's '86 Pontiac Bonneville to the canal where we knew our father had been shooting. He wasn't there, but we stayed.

He'd been taking photos of local boys jumping off the old locks and into the canal below. He had shots of them climbing the steel sides and shots of them ribbing one another to jump in and cool action shots of them mid-flight. Their bodies, in the action shots, were mostly blurs, like streaks of color headed into the water. We wanted to see it because we were drawn to risk taking and wanted to see our father's subjects in action.

We parked in a lot off the highway and walked the mile until we reached the lock where we knew they'd be. We'd heard stories about boys jumping off and hitting their heads on the way down, misjudging and knocking themselves out on the huge metal structures and drowning in the dark water below. I told Jeff about a guy our age, in his early twenties, who was drunk and alone and jumped when the water was low and got stuck in the mud. They found his body after they drained the canal for the winter, or so the story went. I thought it was urban legend, maybe one of those stories you'd tell another guy to scare him before jumping.

The boys there told us that sometimes, when they were underwater, they saw the ghosts of canal diggers that died while digging the ditch. They said our father came to capture their jumping and the ghosts.

The boys climbed the steel girders and we followed, sitting up top with them and watching them jump one after the other. We smoked and made small talk and some of the boys started to wonder if we were going to jump. One of them, the youngest, probably thirteen or fourteen told us how scared he was his first time and how when he hit the water he thought he'd never come up. He said those were the longest and most important seconds of his life. I wasn't sure what he meant, but I think throwing their bodies into the water without knowing how they'd land is sort of like our father and his camera and the need that represents. Often a photographer carries with him some form of regret.

The regulars each had their own stories about jumping. There were a group of them who had been at it years, had seen other boys die, had taken their jumping to new levels by building a plank, rigging a tower on top of the lock – adding height to their jumps, jumping with their feet or hands tied.

Jeff and I were quiet the whole time. The way we knew to be when someone was telling a story. The way we were when we were considering something like jumping into the canal. I took my brother's silence to mean he was jumping, because he was rarely quiet, was more often a flash of energy like the boys' bodies in my father's action shots, a streak of light. My brother who stood at six-foot four inches. His nose bent from hockey fights and years of my pulling on it when we were kids, who looked, at the right angle and unshaven, so much like our father even without glasses on. Jeff handed me his sneakers and stood up. The boys were silent now, which was different for them too, because usually they were all jokes and cheering. But, they sensed, like I did, that this wasn't a normal jump, that my brother was jumping because of our father or maybe because he wanted to see those ghosts.

He threw himself out and away from the metal. He pulled his legs up towards his chest. He hollered like it was the last thing he'd ever do. His scream was a release and it sent the boys, myself included, to cheering.

When he came up after hitting the water, his oversized fists raised toward the sky, beads of water glistening on his shaven head, screaming and hollering along with me who was still high up on the lock, and the boys, who had jumped in after him, I saw that this was my brother's way of communicating with our father of sharing something with him.

My brother and my father don't exchange letters or photographs.

In the car I had a growing list of places my father had taken pictures: *The Laundromat*, Baptist Churches, the abandoned aqueduct where homeless men and women ride out the winter months. There were more, a half dozen: boxing matches, those boys at the canal, the bar we drank at.

I didn't know how people felt about having my father around. How could they trust him, an outsider with a camera? A middle-aged man with worn clothes and big crooked glasses? How did he work his way into these small communities no one else was paying attention to, how did he find them, what was it that drew him to them?

I didn't jump in the canal but climbed down the girders to give Jeff his shoes. We drove home with the windows rolled down but without music and without talking. Still, I sensed the urge to shout bubbling in my brother's throat. I felt it too.

My father was home when Jeff and I got back from the canal. Spread out on his floor were hundreds of photographs. He was sorting through them to determine which were the best. "It's all for the 'Representations of the City' contest," he said. I could see that he wanted his photos to be of places rarely seen or of people who had been overlooked. With his disposable cameras he'd captured people in poverty, sipping forties from paper sacks. Black communities praying for the dead and the dying. Bands who would only play once. Those without money. Without food. Those just simply without.

I found myself thinking about Kodak, all those flashbulbs, and shutters, and negatives. The layoffs. How their factories had lined the city and were now being demolished. Kodak was like a dying beast, falling to its knees right in front of our eyes. Gutted from the inside out, then torn limb from limb. It was as if my father felt he could capture it all, the decay of the city, that emptiness left by the outline of missing structures, and the hope, too, the way his pictures spoke to loss and tried to fill it.

I know about the river. In the summer months my friends and I congregated there, like the boys at the canal. Along its shores, on the docks, in the cattails, on board the abandoned tugboat, we are having fires and telling stories and losing our virginity. We are snapping off our own photos, because this is a place we don't bring our father, and we are finding pieces of the city washed up on the muddy banks. We leave behind beer bottles and cigarette butts. We leave behind footprints and ashes and hidden things of importance like sleeping bags or lighter fluid.

On the old tugboat we find unsent letters from crewmen to wives and children. We find cassette tapes with the music they were listening to when their boat went out of commission; *Primus* and *Alice in Chains* and other music that we broadcast into the night. We find baseball cards from that time period, mostly Mets players, Darryl Strawberry, Gary Carter, Doc Gooden. There are half empty cans of coffee and other foodstuffs. From the banks we drag in empty bottles, which might outnumber the fish. We find toys: dolls and stuffed bears and even a bike that is good save a flat tire, which we can fix and ride along dirt paths. We are the gods of lost things. And, it is important to us, the collection of rejected or lost or discarded items. It is a form of preservation, of storytelling. We take pleasure in reading the letters men wrote to their women, though we— at first— feel guilty, when they talk about months without sex or a growing sense of loss with every mile they travel, with every second they spend away.

A photographer is a kind of collector.

Collecting is easy and exciting. With only flashlights and the light reflected off the clouds from the city, we search the banks and cattails. We have prizes for best item found or a punishment, doled out in drinks or dares, for worst. We chase one another through the woods behind the zoo and snap pictures of one another in different states of fear or elation. We avoid the water. We are afraid of it, won't swim in it, though it is tempting.

We hang our pictures in the bunk area next to those of the crew. We take down the sign, hanging from the platform, which named the boat, "Cheyenne II," and put it at our campsite. We pretend that we are captaining the boat, that we are its crew—even when we're too old for such games—and that when we are not here we're on leave or docking at some exotic port. We have hundreds of photographs from those years, housed on that boat, hidden there, like a keepsake or secret. The boat is a floating monument to our boyhood, a collage of things lost and found in the river, a safe house holding us, forever, above the water.

The sound of trains echoes in the air. Their brakes squeal and their horns sound. Standing near them is like standing on the edge of the locks at the canal, the air swirling, sucking you towards them, the immense power they represent as both a fading technology and an icon. My brother and I toss rocks aimlessly into the train yard as we walk through it toward the river to look for our father.

It is good to walk through the yard, to feel the wind and the dust run through our hair as the cars flash by. I can stand there for minutes on end watching a set of cars pass, imagining the places they're going and the cargo they are carrying; they race off to cities I have never been to and I wish sometimes that I could join them; it's like the tugboat, and those imagined lives we had when we were there—it reminds me of the seriousness of loss.

We get on towards the river, putting bottle caps from our pockets—to be crushed by the trains as souvenirs—on the tracks. My father's friends, a couple of old fishermen, are fishing, poles pointed toward the river, sitting on their old living room furniture. They look peaceful, I think, content in ways most people are not. They live in the syrup factory with my father and this is their living room, they joke. They keep the furniture, which is weather worn and rotting, by the river year round so they can fish in comfort anytime they please.

They're drinking Genny beer in 16oz bottles, which my friends and I call pounders. It's what old men from Rochester drink. Local beer. Sold cheap. They've fashioned end tables and foot rests from empty cases turned yellowish from the rain and the sun. There are cases lying all over the place. My brother and I each take one and sit with them. They ask what my brother and I are up to on this August night. I point back towards the factory. Jeff pulls a six-pack from a plastic bag. "Sitting by the river and having a drink," I say. Which means, waiting for our father, or causing trouble. Or, means just come to see how the fish are biting.

I don't, when I think of a city, think of these people, people with very little who are content with that. That is, I think about poverty and culture and traffic and pollution and crime, of course crime, which everyone is worried about. After all we spend good money to prevent it, to process DNA, to solve murders and rapes and thefts. It's what politicians and police forces and the local news are concerned with, spend most of their time writing speeches about or broadcasting. I don't often think about a few old men fishing from a rotting couch, a middle-aged man in a 12' by 10' room filled with his own photographs, how satisfying that can be. Unless I sit on old cases of beer and try fishing, even though nothing is biting. I find out a lot by sitting near the river with old men who are drinking pounders. I understand what it means to live without TV. Though they have one, resting on a rock, that doesn't have a screen. I learn to appreciate silence, to grow comfortable with it. I hear things when I'm quiet that I would otherwise neglect. Animals moving in the forest. Traffic from the highway. Wind through the canopy. Fish jumping. The waterfall, though it is a mile down river, wearing away at rock. Things that might go overlooked or unheard otherwise.

The more time a photographer spends studying a subject, the more he will ultimately be able to get out of his photographs, the more complex they become.

"Grab a pole, fella, and join us," one of the men says, noticing me eyeing the poles. The one I grab is plastic, a little kid's pole, and it says "Jr. Fisherman" on it. I steal a worm from the Styrofoam cup resting near the poles.

"Have we caught anything today?"

"No, we're in a bit of a drought. Nothing on the line in three days."

We sit there, quiet for a while, hoping the silence will end their dry streak. The sun is setting, the shadows of trees on the other side of the river look like they're dancing on the surface of the water. Jeff doesn't fish but sits in front of the broken television, his feet propped on a fallen limb, his back pressed into a tree.

Something catches on my line and I am nervous. I don't want to be the one to break the streak. I just wanted to have a beer. I want to offer the rod to one of the men sitting on the couch, but I'm not sure about the rules, if a fisherman is supposed to bring in his own catch or if offering would be impolite. I haven't fished in a long time, and when I was fishing my father would bait the hook, cast for me, help me reel my catch in.

"He's got something," one of the men says, noticing the tension of the line.

"Reel it in boy."

My brother stands up. He looks a bit stunned at first, as if he had been watching something on the TV, which he may very well have been. He rushes over to me. There is an excitement in the air now, like whatever is on my line is going to bring good luck, like three days without fish are about to come to an end and somehow we'll all be happier for it. "Don't pull too hard," someone advises. "Nice and easy."

The fight, if you could call it that, feels like it lasts until the sun finally goes down, which may not have been so long since it was already going down. And when I pull it out of the water we're standing there in darkness, my brother pressed close to me, the old men off the couch and moving in to see what we've got.

"It's a freaking boot," I say.

You'd think, with the dry streak alive that everyone would be disappointed, like me. But, Jeff is on the ground laughing. "It took you that long to pull in a boot." His beer is rolling toward the river, headed in to replace what I've pulled out, and he is laughing uncontrollably.

"Now, that is one mighty fine catch," one of the men says. "That is the way to break a dry spell."

"It is?" I say.

But he isn't paying any attention to my question. He's unhooking the catch. "Look at this work boot. You mind if I keep it?"

"No," I say. "Not in the least."

He's already got it off the hook and is heading over to a spot in the dirt where the two old men will build their fire for the night.

"What are you going to do with it?" Jeff asks, as he gets to his feet.

"I'm going to dry it out. What else?"

"Well, what are you going to do with it then?"

I'm secretly wondering the same thing. It does seem like a good boot, despite its having been pulled from the river and all, but what is he going to do with just one?

"I suppose I'm going to have to keep fishing until I find its mate." Both fishermen laugh at this and it seems funny to me too. My brother looks at me and we smile, reach into our six-pack and sip at new beers, return to our original seats. The old men return to the couch. We are on the banks of the Genesee fishing for a boot.

After a while Jeff and I decide to leave and see if our father is home yet.

We pick up our crushed beer caps on the way back and throw more rocks out into the night.

My mother, after my father moves into the syrup factory, tells us that our father loves us, that his photos and his letters are his way of saying that. My mother is a nurse and she thinks she can heal everything, or more likely she feels she must. I tell her that my father's photographs mean more than just love, that they are also about loss. I read it in a book about photography I tell her. A photographer is a student of the world around him. Anyone can capture an image; the photographer is out to capture something more.

We get to the factory, crushed bottle caps in hand, and find our father there. He is sitting at his window, looking down on us, and smoking a cigarette. We go up and he has water boiling on the hot pot. He has a fresh basket of tomatoes on the floor. He smiles. "Where are we headed tonight?"

We tell him about the boot and our fishing expedition. We each have an ear of corn. We decide to meet friends at a bar just down from The Klassy Cat.

Outside the bar there are more posters of the boy who was recently shot, though they are weather worn, surrounded by others: signs for lost pets, signs advertising items for sale. My

father, once we've settled in, asks the bartender if she's heard
anything about that boy's killers and she says she hasn't and is
pretty sure she won't.

"People should be more careful when they're out in the city
alone," she says.

Perhaps she's right. Perhaps murder is a crime that victims can
prevent. Maybe it is a matter of being smarter, of being luckier
somehow. But I don't think my father agrees. His shots of us that
night, posing for him, pool cues raised like we're in sword fights,
the bartenders pretending to flash him, cannot stop murder or
death, are not a means by which to prevent either.

The deadline for the "Representations of the City" contest
passes. I know because I've written it down and kept it in my
wallet. My father doesn't submit his photos, but picks out his
best and places them in an album, and when we visit, he shows
them to us again and again. Sometimes I want to tell him that
nothing is going to bring back that boy who was murdered, or
his marriage, or the ghosts of the canal diggers, but I don't.
Because, we have come to believe in this form of grieving.

LETTER FROM MY FATHER

Sept. 24th, 2007

Jonathan,

It's a strange feeling, one of my sons being gone, living without your mother and the sounds and smells of our house. Now, twenty-one floors from the ground, everything seems eerily quiet, like the world outside my window is just a painting there for my amusement, there to remind me of the world I once came from. From here I can see Kodak Park and the skyline and on clear days I can even see as far as the lake. It's amazing how, from this height, everything about the city I thought I knew takes on a new shape.

The other day, looking down on 104, I saw a deer jump out into rush hour traffic. I don't know how but it made it through unscathed. And, no cars wrecked. It was like some beautifully designed dance, choreographed by the gods, and I felt like one of them looking down on this scene that not so many people got to see or will ever get to see in their lives. I don't know what to make of it, that there is hope in the world or dumb luck. Probably some hunter will get it during deer season, which might only stand to prove that the world is full of comic irony, but that might be the pessimist in me talking.

I have been taking pictures of the city. I feel at home when I am out taking shots of other people or of old places I once knew well. Maybe I'm trying to replace your mother or trying to replace the noise. It isn't all bad here, there are plenty of characters in the building, but the noise of this place is different, maybe more haunting than anything else. There are televisions and radios and the sounds of life, but too there is the sound of death, crying and oxygen tanks and the squeaky wheels on wheelchairs. Like life and death are in a very close proximity to one another.

I've sent you some of my favorite photographs. I hope you like them. Or, I hope you see something that motivates you in them. Your mother tells me, when I call, that you seem to be doing alright, but that maybe you are a bit lonely. This reminds me of how our lives have become so similar, how even though you are my son I can not stop you from feeling pain or pretend any longer that I am impervious to it. I think about us being alone and then think about me living this high off the ground and you in your basement apartment. It seems like an appropriate image or whatever you might call it.

Anyhow, I won't keep you. I'm sure you're busy trying to carve out a place for yourself. Don't be afraid to come home or call when you need something. When I went away during the war my father wrote me and it was one of the few things that brought me comfort. You're going to change and that is all right. It doesn't mean you've sold out or lost your sense of home. I'm proud of you. It means you're growing up.

Dad

X-RAY

Pony's arm looks like it's going to fall off, looks like a raw cut of meat, like something from a sci-fi movie. I've told him to go to the doctor but he doesn't have health insurance and can't afford the bills. He's living in his car outside of the KFC he's working at. It's his doping arm and he's worried about HIV. I'm worried about gangrene. Either way he can barely move it. "They're going to want to x-ray it," he says. "And I don't like that thing. It scares me." What scares him is the image, the photograph of the bone, the fact that it can see through his skin. I don't tell him but I have a collection of x-ray pictures, which my mother has gotten for me from the hospital she works at. I collect them because I am fascinated by their ability to see things. I wish I could see like that. I wish I could tell the future the way Pony imagines the x-ray does, so I can warn him or stop him or something.

We're under the walking bridge drinking forties and heckling people as they walk over us. Pus oozes from Pony's arm and blood, too. "Will you go to the Hotel Cadillac with me?" he asks. Which isn't a hotel anymore but a clinic where he can get tested for HIV. I tell him I'll go. I'll even get tested if he wants.

We get quiet because we hear a couple talking above us. The boy is telling the girl how much he loves her and respects her and all those other lies boys tell girls in order to get their fingers down her pants or when they want her hand down theirs.

"Have some respect, man," Pony says. "Tell her what you really want."

And I say, "Come down here honey and we'll show you love."

We laugh at our own stupid jokes. Me, who will move away to college in a few months, who will run away from this place, who will guess at what Pony is in for and never say a word.

"Fuck you, man," the kid shouts. "I'll kick your fucking ass."

"It's going to be hard from up there, pal," Pony says. We taunt him because we know he won't come down, know that it will take him too much time, that climbing out under here always involves risk.

"Come down here and make me respect you," I say.

They move on but not without more minor threats, the girl ending it by calling us assholes. When they're gone we get quiet. Pony plays at slipping like he's going down toward the river, as if he knows he's headed in, bound for it, sooner or later, now or three months from now. It's early in the summer; motorboats zoom by underneath us carrying women without tops on, fishermen with cases of beer and cans of worms. Pony's face is all sweat because it's warm under the bridge and because of the pain in his arm and because of the beer we're drinking.

We don't stay under there much longer, but head topside instead. This is the bridge where handfuls of kids will get their bikes stolen this summer, where kids our age, with more energy and a more cruel sense of humor, will take them. It's the bridge that separates the city from the suburbs, the bridge families come out on after trips to the zoo, which is down the road, to see the river and Kodak's buildings and the Rochester skyline.

A family of four walks by and gives us a dirty look. The

father seems like he wants to say something to us, but seeing Pony's arm or how sick he looks the man decides against it. I think every place knows loss like this. Pony puts his forty down and picks at the hole in his arm. "Hotel Cadillac," I say, pointing towards the city side of the river where we'll have to catch a bus and a transfer to get there, but there will be air conditioning—some form of relief. And we both stand, launching our near empty bottles over the railing and into the river below.

They fall without caring what they hit.

THE WORLD BEFORE THIS ONE

In March of 1988, Arthur Shawcross
began murdering prostitutes in the Rochester area,
claiming 11 victims before his capture two years later.
His victims were usually strangled and battered
to death, and were often mutilated as well.
Most of them were found near the Genesee River.

He is out there and he is coming. They will, well after you're dead, call him the Genesee River Killer. All serial killers get names.

It is 1988 and I am sleeping at my best friend's house. I am eight years old. You aren't coming home. They won't catch this man, this killer, not for another two years. Everyone in my grade school finds out. At ten, I am reminded of your body found in the river. Every night I see you floating and moving in the current, a piece of driftwood, eaten away by the river teeth.

This is not some childhood nightmare about monsters, is not residue from a scary movie. I am writing from the future, writing with the voices of my classmates in my head, who knew, who whispered it in the hallways and on the playground. "Murdered." I have reread the headlines and you are still there. He comes at night. March 3rd, 1988. It is cold and the streets are dusted with snow. He brings you to the river, drags you through the woods and muddy banks. He is a fisherman. He knows the places to hide and knows where to go so he can take his time. He will have his way with you, cut you like something pulled from the water, like some piece of prey on the end of a line.

Erase every misstep that leads you to the water or puts you in harm's way. Don't work at night when the traffic is heavy and the "John's" come more willingly. Don't think arming yourself will save you. Don't think the police are going to stop this. They have refused to hear me, have turned away my letters of warning.

Warn the girls you work with. Because, you are first. He is going to kill eleven of them, including you. And do this for me: go back to school. Move in with friends. Visit the art gallery. Go to the zoo. Get caught stealing from the public market and spend a night, this one night in 1988, in jail. Grow a garden and spend your time tending it. Buy a big house in a suburb. Paint it metallic blue or pink to piss off the neighbors. Marry for money. Have affairs. Buy lottery tickets. Show up in my class when I am ten. Show everyone that you aren't dead.

I cannot stop him. I'm only here to warn you: he is coming like a thunderstorm that does not announce itself, soaks all the clothes hanging on the line, traps people out walking their dogs, fills our shoes, yours and mine, so full of water that we are forever wet to the bone.

UNDERTOW

I. Mausoleum

Aiden braces himself against the branches of a tree as he walks down the embankment. The ground is covered with leaves and melting frost, the after effects of a cold November night. He balances himself against the incline, his feet sliding out with the leaves, trying to keep from dropping the twelve pack of Genny Cream Ale he's brought with him. Looking through the dim dawn light, he sees the mouth of the cave, sees the bodies of dead fish, their frozen carcasses thawing with the rising sun. When he reaches the cave, he kicks one of the bodies, watches it roll over from one side to the other, its eyes eaten out by birds or decay. He nudges it with his foot towards the water; its body as it once was, returning to the river.

He moves forward walking in zigzags to avoid the hordes of fish stretching from the shoreline to the back of the cave. The fish seem fresher, less eaten away at by the sun and scavengers, as he moves toward the back, as he switches on his flashlight and escapes the sound of the waterfall and the river.

When Aiden reaches the pitch dark, when all he can see is a small trace of the morning, he finds the entrance, a hole in the rock structure, a door so small he has to get down on his hands and knees sliding fish out of his way so he can crawl through it. He's got a good pile of fish, five or ten on each side of the door now, and looks closely at their silvery bellies swollen with eggs or their last meal or their last breath. The cave and his stack of fish remind Aiden of a mausoleum, of some sort of mass fish grave, makes him think about family and all that comes with that.

Aiden's older brother killed himself this summer jumping off the walking bridge in Seneca Park. All his friends are pretty sure it was a suicide but the paper doesn't say anything except for the obit, which is short and has Aiden's name in it as someone who Pony is survived by. What Aiden wants is to see how it played out, like a movie or like one of those short films at the peep booths they used to go to. Did his brother jump headfirst or cannonball style the way he did when they'd go swimming? Is it possible while climbing on the steel underbelly of the bridge that he simply fell? Was Pony alive when he hit the water or dead? And if he wasn't dead, what was under there in the dark, in that current that carries things like a freeway traveled by wrappers and animals and lost things?

Aiden carries the obit folded in his wallet. He unfolds it, the ink smeared and the creases wearing through, and searches for some answers in the official air of it, in its attention to facts and dates. He has run his thumb over his own name so many times that it is erased from the text.

When he found out, he walked down to the bridge where he knew Pony had jumped, crawled out under it and collected the few trinkets they had left there. He sat over one of the 2' by 2' openings and dropped the trinkets down one at a time, their Bert and Ernie figurine, which their mutual crush had given them. And other things: empty bottles, one for each beer they'd tried, and the KFC regalia they'd stolen from Pony' job, baseball caps and polo shirts and boxes of honey mustard and barbecue sauce, which they'd eaten in handfuls when they were high or just on dares. Aiden watched all of it vanish below the surface of the water, leaving behind tiny splashes like a leaky ceiling into a bucket before being swept under, before disappearing.

Aiden's stepfather tried to talk to him after Pony's death, tried to tell him that suicide was an imbalance in someone that no other person could erase. Like a mistake. Something nature didn't intend. It didn't help and Aiden had nothing to say.

Aiden got Pony's car, a rusted out red Ford Tempo, from the KFC parking lot— they were going to impound it, but his mother went down and told them they weren't touching her son's car without hearing from her lawyer and they let her have it because they were city cops and city cops always have other things to worry about. Aiden imagines it, a parking lot full of abandoned cars, homeless people like his brother sleeping in them, little Hoovervilles on wheels, he thinks and smiles.

Pony's car is parked, dead in their stepfather's backyard. The stepfather who insisted their mother throw Pony out because of the drugs and the stealing and all the other crimes he'd committed. The car is out behind the garage where his mother can't see it from the kitchen. Their stepfather says it is a constant reminder of her dead son and she shouldn't be looking at it. Aiden spends hours in it. He drinks out there and runs the battery listening to the oldies station, which was Pony's favorite, bands like The Four Tops and The Temptations, the things they'd seen their parents dance to, the music they remember as background for family pictures and holidays before their real dad's death and the subsequent stepfather. One day their mother came out and sat down next to Aiden, listened for a while to the music her oldest son listened to and she asked Aiden to dance. It had only been a few days since they'd buried Pony. Aiden and his mother looked like a Polaroid picture, standing in a field in front of a broken down Ford Tempo, like a postcard never mailed and never read.

When officer Tantillo came to their house, Aiden was the only one home. He knew when he saw Tantillo that it wasn't good news because he was the narcotics officer that ran the D.A.R.E program at their school and he'd been involved in a few of Pony's prior arrests. Tantillo asked Aiden if he wanted to go to the station to identify the body or wait for his parents. He decided he'd wanted to go without them. When they got to the morgue, it was nothing like Aiden had expected, all bright and warm and sort of lived in. There were fast food wrappers on one of the counters and someone's shoes, perhaps removed for comfort, lying on the floor. A pretty girl sat at a desk with a list of names or numbers, too pretty, Aiden thought, to be in a place like this with her deep red lipstick and freckled skin.

Aiden, once officer Tantillo had left him with the girl who would take him to the body, couldn't bring himself to go in. He was afraid of her, of how much he fell in love with her upon seeing her and didn't want to hate her when she brought him to the body of his older brother. He wasn't certain of Pony's death, though Tantillo would know as well as him or his parents what Pony looked like, and he didn't want certainty, especially not in front of that girl. He walked home, stopping by the KFC to see if Pony was there, parked in his car, listening to oldies or maybe even taking out the trash or having a smoke break. Aiden went home and sat behind the shed where his brother's car would be parked in a few days, waiting for his parents to come home, to go to the police station themselves, to return with news.

Aiden looks at the fish lying all around the little side cave he's crawled into, looks up at the bags nailed into the wall full of their things: found toys, bottles, squirt guns. Normally Pony would be here with him once the water had drained out for the winter and they'd clean out the room, take the bags down and set up their things, creating, for the cold months, a hideout. Inside they'd lay rocks from the river for a fire pit, would put lamps with candleholders in them around the room. He turns his attention to the fish, stands around them, in the middle of them, unsure of what to do. He opens one of the beers from his twelve pack, sips it, carefully breaks the tab off for good luck, making sure not to bend it or damage the can. He kicks at the fish in front of him, their bodies slamming against the wall or sliding through the opening into the main cave, his beer splashing onto his hand, his mind telling them to swim before the water subsides and they're all left flopping on dry land, dead.

He slams his beer against the far wall and thinks of Officer Tantilo's advice when they were in D.A.R.E, about all the advice that people have for him now that his brother is dead.

Feeling suddenly dizzy, he sits down amongst the fish, knowing that he'll carry their scent for the rest of the day. He notices the flashlight—which rests on the floor—its beam reflecting off the shiny scales and scattering around the room. He looks right into the beam so intensely that the room and the fish and the bags of things disappear. He loses himself like this, looking at light bulbs or television screens. He thinks these "spells" (what the doctor called them) have to do with loss or absence or something his mother said after their

father died so many years ago. But then another part of him
thinks it is some sort of disorder or way of understanding the
world, which he hasn't yet named or figured out.

Aiden remembers the night he and Pony both lost their
virginity. They were in Pony's car, Pony up front and Aiden
in the back. They'd gone on a double date with the Carter
sisters and they were making out with them down behind the
zoo. Rumor had it that if you could get one of them to do
something, give you a hand job, go down on you, you could
get the other to do the same with your buddy. Pony had been
dating the older one, Nikki, and he knew that if he got her
to sleep with him for the first time while her sister was there
with his brother, then they'd both have a chance. Aiden can
see Pony from the back seat, even though the younger sister,
Shannon, is on top of him, kissing at his neck. In the rearview
he sees Nikki taking his brother's penis in her mouth, sees
his brother's hands pushing up and down on her head. In the
light coming down the hill from the zoo, he can't make out
their features, knows nothing except that they are young and
passionate and together. Aiden is no longer paying attention
to his date, his eyes, as she unbuttons his pants, are glued to
the light, the way it wraps around the branches and leaves of
the trees overhead, watches as everything freezes and all four
of them are naked and alive and almost lost in the dark.

Aiden moves around the cave in a slow circle. Pony found this
place three winters ago on a fishing expedition. He brought
his friend Big Bear and his little brother here to establish a
fort. The three of them drank bottles of Genny Light in the
dark, occasionally flipping on a lighter to find another bottle
or to light a smoke. Then when their eighteen-pack was gone,
they smashed the bottles against the back wall of the larger
cave, risking their flesh and the possibility of injury with

every shattered bottle that resonated out into the darkness. Aiden returned after the first snowfall alone with a six-pack of expensive beer his stepfather had left in the fridge. He smashed the bottles in the smaller cave where the glass and the liquid sprayed up around him and left his arms covered in small cuts and his pants soaked through. When he turned on his flashlight, he could see one last fish flopping in the remaining water that hadn't evaporated yet, broken bits of bottle imbedded in its scales.

Alone again, Aiden remembers the sound of those bottles breaking, hears it filling the air around him. It's quiet at first and then grows louder, drowning out the sound of the waterfall and the river and the other sounds that occur in the silence of the cave. He remembers their first trip here, the way the water hadn't completely drained yet, the way his feet were cold and his heart raced as pools of fish flopped around them. He wishes he'd had a picture of it, them splashing around in the dark, excited with the promise of escape.

It's getting on toward noon now, and he looks down at the floor, which is completely dry, and he is sure he must rebuild the cave, take down their things and gently carry the fish to the water. He picks up the first fish, begins the clean up by running his hands over its slimy scales, to remember the way it makes him feel being this close to death. He sits down in the pile again and begins sliding the fish with care towards the tiny opening into the larger cave.

Aiden used to go to different Catholic churches for Saturday Mass. He would sneak in five minutes late and sit in the last pew, being sure to slide slowly into his seat, and he would watch, not the Mass so much as the people, the regulars, who he'd come to know by sight and then the people who came once a month or once every few months. He liked to see how they reacted, whether they sang during the hymns or knew the prayers. He could tell who was faking by the way they moved their mouth or the way their head was positioned. He'd been a faker once, had mumbled the few words he'd known, and most of his prayers asked God to make sure no one knew he was faking, but he'd come to learn all the common ones, all the ones a once a month member or maybe even twice a month member might know. He remembers one time an older woman fell when she tried to move toward the kneeler and then the whole service stopped and women rushed to her. He remembers laughing and the whole congregation looking back at him, noticing—he imagined—his presence for the first time. In his mind everything was frozen but his laughter, which played on like a soundtrack despite the movie's end, the credits scrolled through. The sound of it echoes and everyone is looking at him and he cannot stop.

He liked Confirmation the most although he'd never taken part in it. He felt moved by the order of it, the ceremony. Sometimes he'd sneak in before Mass and confess, telling the priest that he wanted to take part in the Confirmation but had not been through Communion and felt guilty about it. He confessed that he didn't understand that guilt because he had stolen and lied before but for some reason couldn't bring himself to do this one very simple and perhaps less offensive act. Aiden wanted the priest to tell him it was all right to come up for Confirmation, but none of them ever did and he always thought that unchristian.

Before his brother's death, Aiden and Pony collected holiday lawn ornaments. Right before Christmas, in November and early December, when people are putting up decorations through the suburbs, they sneak out at night in fresh snow after blizzards and load them into Pony's Ford Tempo, the head of Santa Claus or the antlers of Rudolph hanging out the open back window. They have a place along the river where they can steal electric from one of Kodak's outlet buildings, can plug the light up ones in, where they've created a holiday land of their own. There is an island carved into the cattails and swampy area around the river where all sorts of Santa Claus pieces and three nativity scenes and dozens of Frosty the Snowman figures glow out at passing boats. They use their stepfather's rowboat, with its small outboard motor, as a way to complete their delivery. This thievery is something Aiden holds close to him, like their own way of celebrating the holidays or making them meaningful. He and Pony have a lighting ceremony every year where they bring all their friends out, five at a time, in the boat on the 22nd of December, motoring the ten minutes to the island where they make the shore ignite like a gaudy Neverland, like the cattails are on fire or, if the lights are blinking, like a bunch of flashbulbs firing out and into the night.

Aiden likes to paddle out to the middle of the river once the lighting has taken place and look in on his friends, on his brother and their creation. Sometimes he takes a girl with him, but mostly he goes alone every night for the two weeks they do it, and he sits there smoking a cigarette and gawking at the whole thing like a little kid believing in the possibility of reindeer and elves and the North Pole. He can barely make out the forms of the ornaments from the river, can't determine what his friends are saying, their screams and laughter blending together to form some kind of Christmas carol. This always makes him think of his father, of going to the Christmas service at St. Margaret Mary's, of the year they had two trees because his dad wanted the gaudy silver fake tree and their mother wanted a real one.

They sink each year's lawn ornaments after the holiday in a "sacrifice" to the river. Aiden can't wait, as they sink the old ones, for next Christmas and the ornaments they'll have then, can't wait to see what stuff stores will be peddling.

Aiden has, since his brother's death, tried to imagine years of their holiday offerings bumping along the bottom of the river and being dragged out to the lake. He sees them catching in pockets, areas where the river eddies or on sand bars in the lake. He thinks of these places, the eddies and sandbars, the way he imagines his cave and the safety and comfort it brings him even without his brother. He imagines the river eating away at the plastic, chipping away first the paint, and then whole sections of the figures, pieces of them floating to the surface, polished white, the hint of things dead and disposed of, the hint of things hidden in the river.

But now Aiden crawls toward the small opening into the larger cave. He puts his hands against the collected mass of fish he's made, forming a barrier between him and the outside cave. Aiden pushes hard, driving the collected bodies forward; as he stands now in the larger opening, he looks at his hands, dripping with water and fish slime. He bends down after wiping his hands on his pants and picks up the first bunch. He moves toward the river with great care like a child holding cartons of eggs.

Mist from the waterfall sprays Aiden as he bends toward the river. He looks over at it, marvels at its power, endless and deadly. There are fishermen on the other shore, and Aiden watches as they cast and then pull their lines in and then cast again, creating perfect, unbroken arches. When the line and bait hit the water they are followed by a slight splash, which shoots randomly toward the air and lands again.

Everything returns to the river.

II. This Close to the Possibility of Death

Aiden remembers being locked in a dark space, pressed in amongst old mothball smelling shirts and suit jackets in his father's closet. He is waving his arms around, trying to find the door, but its dark and he can't orient himself amongst the clothes and the smell. Pony is outside the door giggling as he listens to the sound of the plastic that covers the clothing, listens to Aiden whimper and struggle.

"You're going to stop crying," Pony says.

Aiden slams himself into the door jarring it forward momentarily against the weight of his brother who is holding it shut on the other side. Pony bounces back for a second and then slams his shoulder into the door, pushing Aiden into the clothing and hangers.

"Dad's dead. And you're going to stop crying," Pony says. "Men don't cry."

Aiden stops moving, sits on the floor, still hiccupping a little. "Fuck you."

"Say you'll stop crying and I'll let you out."

Aiden focuses on one of the shirts in front of him, letting his eyes adjust to the dark. This is the first time that the world goes on pause, where everything in the room, the plastic swaying as he breathes on it, the sound of Pony slumped against the door outside, tapping with his finger—they all stop and the only thing Aiden notices is that shirt and the dust that has started to collect on it. Aiden wants to yell at his brother, point out the dust collecting on their father's clothing. He counts in his head. Fourteen days, he thinks, we are still so close to his death and their mother is still crying and Aiden just wants to be able to as well. But he also wants very desperately to get out of this closet, which he thought might smell like his father but doesn't and won't ever again.

III. Sick Room

Aiden thinks back to when he was fourteen and his father was dying. He sees himself walk into the pantry at his grandparents' house and feels his mother's arms around him, her warm tears pooling on his shoulder and soaking into his T-shirt. His eyes are frozen on the canned goods lining the walls, a can of Campbell's Soup reading, "It Cures;" a whole world of sustenance incapable of healing anything, he thinks. He remembers the smell of laundry detergent and the sound of the washer drowning out his mother's sobs. He remembers the light seeping in from the hallway and voices, his relatives, talking about football or the weather, everything but what they're all thinking about—his father's impending death— which is hanging over the house, oozing from the room he lies in, where he refuses meals and is too weak to get out of bed. It waits like a stranger at the door with his finger pressed to the peephole.

Aiden wants to talk to his father, wants to ask him questions about school and girls, which he is—sort of—starting to notice, wants his father to eat meals so they can do son stuff like play catch or camp. But his father cannot. When the family, aunts and uncles and grandparents, are all sitting in the dining room eating Thanksgiving dinner, looking in on his father's bed, his father sits up with a tray of food in front of him. His mother—Aiden's grandmother—sits with him trying to make him eat, though he refuses. Aiden doesn't say much, watches his father sip at some broth, drink a glass of water. His father quietly, at first, refuses anything else: bread, meat, even a second glass of water. His hands are weak, like the whole of him, but he squeezes his mother's wrist when she pushes too hard, looks at her sternly, the way he might one of his sons, and says "Leave it be." From the dining room, the adults keep pushing him, his father telling him, "Eat, god damn it." His wife, Aiden and Pony's mother, pleading with him. Aiden and Pony exchange a look, each of them feeling a bit betrayed by their father, but even more sorry for him. How he is a child now. He won't be able to keep the meal down. He knows that. And so do they. They've had talks with their father, the two of them, when everyone else is out, shopping for the upcoming holidays or at dinner. They know and he's made it no secret that he will be dead soon. He can't beat his cancer this time. His refusal to eat and their silence is a sort of final secret between them. An alliance in this acceptance of death and its coming.

Aiden imagines his grandfather sitting in the sick bed, wishes him there. For a second, Aiden sees his father sitting at the table with them, making jokes about Pilgrims and Indians and doting on his wife the way he does during the holidays. Aiden begins to doubt the validity of his memory, of any memory where his father is not sick, where he and Pony are not the sons of a dying man. He read in some book on faith or parenting his mother had lying around the house that children who have lost a parent early in life are forever in mourning. Staring in on his father, Aiden realizes for the first time that he is already in mourning, that this condition, this forever, has already taken hold of him. He thinks about the Christmas presents people have purchased for his father, the ones still waiting to be wrapped, or the few, mailed to his grandparents' house early by his brothers and sisters, waiting to be unwrapped. His grandfather is still at work on his father, doing his best bad cop to bully him into eating something. The glass in Aiden's hand falls, hitting the table first and splashing up toward the ceiling; he looks over at Pony, trying to make him understand the reason for his eyes rolling back into his head, the way his body is slumping to the right, headed for the floor. All of it is slow motion. It's all a fake. He just wants his father to be left alone.

IV. Another Kind of Confession

Aiden is walking with Pony in the woods behind the zoo. There are thinly worn trails from people walking their dogs and kids exploring. Pony says he loves the woods, the way the trees grow without direction, the way they take over every inch with their roots and branches and leaves.

Aiden looks into the landscape ahead—the trees resemble a group of giants, their massive legs walking them towards the river. Aiden and Pony are headed there too, have come to get away from their mother and her new boyfriend, their eventual stepfather. It's only been six months since their father's death. And this is in the air between them.

"The only drawback to these woods is the smell of the river," Pony says. Aiden blows smoke rings into the air. "I wonder what makes it smell so fucking bad?"

"Good question," Aiden says, his long hair drawn back by the wind.

"They're probably pouring our shit and piss in it. Plus Kodak is probably still dumping all kinds of garbage into this thing. You can't even swim in this pond."

Aiden shakes his head.

"Besides, who'd want to swim in it? Look when we get down there." Pony points as they start walking down a set of stairs. "All that stuff just collecting on the shore. Can you see it?"

"Yup."

"It's like the river spits it all out, isn't it?"

"Never thought of it like that," Aiden says.

Aiden thinks about it, the water, the way it is their means of transportation and a site of happiness despite how ugly it is. It is a place for them to return to.

Pony points across the river. "See the crane sitting out on that fallen tree?"

Aiden focuses on the far bank. It's done nothing to hide; with its long noble neck hanging out over the water, it looks like a parent guarding the nest.

"I see a lot of those birds when I'm down here," Pony says.

"I wonder what they're doing just sitting there? Getting warm or something?"

"I'm not sure. Maybe waiting for one giant fish to come by so they'll be fed for months." Pony wants to stop talking about the river and the crane, wants the conversation to switch to the boyfriend. It's building, the need to say something, like water in a tub that is about to overflow, like rain in the street when the gutters are clogged. "What do you think of mom's new guy?"

There is the obvious response, but attached are other questions about their father and that mourning which they both know will always be there. "He's a fucking clown."

"Agreed," Pony says, "a real chode." Pony launches a rock out into the water. There's more to talk about, he knows. He'll confess to Aiden that he doesn't miss their father. That he can't bring himself to or something like that. But for now, the brothers sit on the bank skipping rocks.

V. Visiting

Aiden is looking at the directory in front of the Holy Sepulchre Cemetery, searching for the spot. In his right hand he carries the first stolen ornament of the year, taken from the steps at St. Margaret Mary's. His feet kick at small piles of snow along the freshly plowed road guiding him toward the ledge overlooking the Genesee and to the place where his father and brother are buried. He shakes the ornament with both hands, a snow globe probably left on the steps by a child after Sunday school, and watches the world inside blizzard, so engrossed in it that he forgets to pay attention to the path and falls forward into a snow bank, the ornament pitched forward and swallowed by the snow.

Aiden lies there, his face in his hands, elbows locked. His hair leaves brush marks in the powder as he shakes his head, laughing at himself and his lost ornament. Ahead he can see the weeping willow with its sagging branches almost laying its hands on Pony's headstone. It is the only tree near his father and his brother and he likes to think it protects them, watches them. It's seven years now since his father's death, only a few months since his brother's, and this early snow at the end of October is what has made him come. It will be the first time Aiden steals Christmas things on his own and the first time he fixes the cave, which he plans to do soon, in another few weeks when he is sure the water is gone and the fish are all dead. Aiden pulls himself up. He sits in the snow, his feet in the road, dusting off his jacket. He draws a cigarette from his pocket and the crushed pack, lights it, and gets to his feet. He takes a long look at the willow before continuing down the road. Aiden sits at his father's stone, leans against it, his head on the blank side, to the right, where space has been left for his mother's name. He pulls his lighter out again and flicks it on, lets the wind blow it out. Lights it again. He wonders if, despite her new husband, his mother will be buried here, if her name will ever fill this blank space and if it does, which name she will take.

Aiden looks over at Pony, notices the empty plot next to his. Their father, when they were young, bought these four spaces for the family. He was a practical man like that. It bothered their mother. This purchase seemed like a bad omen. And now Aiden thinks she was right. The willow brushes against Pony's headstone and Aiden wonders if the tree knows Pony is in there and alive, trying to save him. It's possible, Aiden thinks, that a mistake was made, that his brother, when pulled from the river, was very much alive and is now wrestling to be free. Don't cry, Aiden thinks and reaches his hand toward the branches. He is on his hands and knees now, in front of Pony's headstone, and he looks like that woman who fell at the Saturday mass. He giggles, his hands in front of him, in mock or maybe even real prayer.

He does not know what his mother will want. He knows he wants to be here.

Aiden, gently lifting himself into place, lies down in the outside plot. He tucks his arms in next to his sides, he snaps his legs together and tries to slow his breathing. He stares off into the top of the willow tree. The few snowflakes falling, the branches swaying in the breeze. And Aiden lies there, slowly covered by the snow.

VI. Returning to the River

Sitting in his stepfather's rowboat with the motor idling, Aiden looks in on the Christmas lighting. He's done it a night early and alone so that he can have this to himself. It is a monstrosity, the type of thing families line up for, drive the long way home to see, pay ungodly amounts of money to walk through. He's dedicated himself this year, stealing two and sometimes three pieces a night. Without the car he carries pieces on his back, drags them along the snow-covered streets, uses an old wagon he's found in the shed as a means of transportation. He's stolen over sixty pieces. Light up ones and blow up ones. This year there are characters from every cartoon series imaginable. And there are older ones, ones from when he was a kid, Rudolph and Frosty and Jack Frost. These are his favorite though he also felt a tinge of guilt when he took them. He has separated all of them into categories and spread them around the island and in the cattails according to this: "true" Christmas, religious, television. It looks like a park. Throughout it pieces stay lit and others flash and finally it glows out into the river and into the city like a gift. Aiden remembers reading about the River Styx, about the way the gods respected it and swore an oath to it. His teacher said the gods who didn't obey the oath drank from the river and lost their voices for nine years, remembers her telling the class that the River Styx had the power to make someone immortal. Aiden removes his brother's obituary from his wallet, puts his hand into the water, and lets it go. Everything begins to freeze. Slow motion. The lights stop blinking and the river stops flowing and the motor's humming fades. Aiden decides, right before it all freezes and before he moves or blinks to unfreeze it, that he's going to keep the Christmas things this year. He is not going to sacrifice anything to the river. Aiden puts his hand on the motor, feels the heat against his bare hand. The lights are blinking again and a Coast Guard boat is coming up the river, the sound of it setting the world in motion. Aiden puts the motor in gear, slides the boat into the tiny channel where it will be hidden in the dark, and climbs into the cattails. He looks from the bank at the passing boat, the faces of the two men who are on it as they stare at his creation filled with a sort of awe and disbelief. As Aiden escapes into the bright lights.

SUM

It's his first thought, Big Bear's, his six foot four inch frame blocking traffic, standing in the middle of St. Paul Blvd., to drop trou, disrobe, to show oncoming vehicles the other reason we call him Big Bear. We're sitting in Ralph's Chevy Blazer. I'm driving, DD for the night. We're parked in the driveway of Bear's mother's house watching Bear make an ass of himself, ten of us jammed into the SUV, sweating against the leather seats with the windows rolled down so we can shout at Bear, the air conditioning on full blast and the radio turned all the way down. Bear has his pants around his ankles, looking like a middle-aged man with his beer gut and jiggling legs. He has his hands on his hips, the fingernails digging into the flesh. He swirls his torso like a blender, like a tornado, like a toilet being flushed. Bear performs the Macarena, does the Hokey Pokey, falling when he turns himself around, recovers into the Y-M-C-A, starts shaking his ass like he's working a pole at The Klassy Cat, like he can rewind the past few weeks and months and maybe even years and grind and gyrate back all the people and things that are gone.

Ralph climbs out and grabs the thirty-pack Bear left on the ground in front of the house before he took a piss on the sidewalk, before he decided to walk out into the road and dance. Some might say that taunting someone who is so clearly drunk with more booze is wrong, that a good friend would walk out there and drag his naked ass into the house and maybe even dunk him in his little brother's kiddy pool for dramatic effect. But this is how you do it, how you coax Bear in when he gets like this. You can't talk to him about his grandmother who just died or his father who died from a brain tumor, not a year before that. You can't talk about Pony, our dead friend who gave himself over to the river. It's not the beer and it's not the heat. It's not that Bear just got fired from Wal-Mart for making a joke that was "sexual in nature," or that his mother is on welfare, that his little brother's feet are caked with mud and dust and ashes from cigarettes. Even Bear himself can't be held accountable for his actions.

There is, however, to Bear's dancing, the sense of order one seeks from grief when one carries it around without access to a solution, where the M follows the Y and the C the M and on and on like that, and the only thing yet to be determined, because the music is in his head and has no definite end point, is when he'll stop, or if he will have the energy to go on dancing forever. There are, of course, variations like falling, spinning, hands in the air, or that John Travolta move, pointing a finger to the sky and back to the hip and back to the sky, but those are like so few things in life: correctable, erasable. There is the heat in the limbs and head, the contortion of the body, the hips moving side to side, the awkwardness of hands and arms, the kinetic transfer from one body to another as skin and sweat collide, those tiny hairs on the arms raised by chill or arousal, swaying back on the balls of the feet, but Bear is alone in the middle of a four lane boulevard and Ralph is coaxing him in, baiting him, despite the obvious pun about bears and trapping, with the leftover beer, the elixir that set our Bear in motion. And I'm looking out on him, swimming through my own sort of drunkenness, and I can smell the river, which is over the railroad crossing and down a steep incline and under the bridge where Pony jumped, not a half mile from here, and I sense the meaning of Bear's dancing, though I can't vouch for his nakedness, can see in every sloppy step the things he's trying to "shake out," "slough off," "silence, once and for all." Bear moves as if it were an offering, an ancient and sacred dance, like a prayer, not for rain or for ghosts so much, but for something we all, those of us sitting in the car watching, laughing, shouting out his name, want but are unable to ask for, and I think as he stumbles around that the only thing keeping Bear on his feet is his refusal to believe us when we tell him "No matter what, there will always be loss," because he knows even we, in our own grief, do not want to believe it.

CORONER'S REPORT

Name of Examiner: Dennis Campbell
Name of Deceased: Michael Burkard
Age Deceased: 23
Sex: Male
Race: Caucasian
Presumed Cause of Death: Drowning
Date and Time Exam Started: 9/3/05, 11:31am
Date and Time Exam Ended: 9/3/05, 2:13 pm

The average time for a human body to cool to the touch is 12 hours. 24 to cool to the core.

The body on this date, September 2nd, 2005, of Michael Burkard was pulled from the Genesee River. No signs of struggle or obvious signs of homicide.

The first evaluation provides no clarity relative to Michael's time of death. His submergence and exposure to the elements in the river (fish, currents, rock formations, etc.) have made it near impossible to determine this.

The age and race of this victim, along with the noticeable absence of traditional homicide related injuries, might suggest suicide.

The boy comes from a middle class family. He is 23. He has no last known address and has listed his 18-year-old brother as his contact in case of emergency.

The body, decomposition aside, shows clear signs of malnutrition.

The body's cells, during drowning, cease aerobic respiration, and are unable to generate the energy needed to maintain normal muscle biochemistry.

The boy's eyes are open, suggesting he was concious at the moment he entered the water, as if he were trying to freeze this moment, capture it forever in the tissue.

The brain cells can die if deprived of oxygen for more than three minutes, thereby eradicating one's memory.

The cause of this drowning may never be determined.

A body in water does not decompose like the rest.

The boy looks content.

The body still waterlogged like my son when I pull him from the bath.

The hair frizzled and clinging to the neck and down onto the shoulders.

The boy, Michael, wearing, prior to examination, a Sesame Street T-shirt. What is that all about, I wonder?

The shirt a gift from some girl or maybe a relative, this eighteen year old brother, who is bound to come here, not so many days or weeks removed from last seeing his older sibling.

The shoes he was wearing were full of holes.

The things I found in his mouth are not an indication of crimes committed.

The boy must have parents.

This body, Michael, is not the first 23-year-old to come in from the river, dragged in like a catfish, but the first to have the tattoo of a pony on his chest.

The sudden feeling that this all means something.

The truth: I stopped, shortly after starting this exam, for lunch.

The kid on this table looks like he might have been nice. The way his eyes and mouth are shaped let me know that.

The hands look like they've been worked, make me think he was not so alone in this world.

The only answer lies herein.

The body: falls, falling, fallen.

The boy, giving himself over to the current.

LETTER TO JEFF, FROM OHIO

November 17th, 2007

Jeff,

I know we haven't talked much since the move. It's hard to explain but I guess I am kind of burying myself here, trying to get comfortable with my loneliness, with my grief.

Some nights I go out and walk for hours. I carry beer in my backpack and packs of those short cigars we smoked when we were kids. Often times I will sit watching the sun set over Columbus and wonder what makes this place different from home. The sounds and the smells, the way I can walk almost anywhere. There isn't one thing or even a handful of things that make it foreign. It just is. And I don't, even though I am learning about the city, mapping it under my feet, feel this deep sense of displacement fading.

I don't know that you know this but Dad sends me letters, or rather photographs with notes written on the back. I think he feels closer to me now that I am gone, now that we are living the same solitary lifestyle. His letters are really beautiful and sad. I worry about him a lot. I am seeing him, in them, for the first time. Sometimes I even find myself wishing Mom would just take him back. You can, in every letter, sense how deeply he regrets not appreciating the life he had, and now that I am away from home I feel this kind of disappointment creeping up on me too.

My greatest fear is that I will let slip away that which I love most. I find myself fighting very hard to remain whole, even though I don't know what that means. I sense myself sabotaging my time here so that it does not creep in, invade me and disconnect me from home. It's scary thinking that I might return and not fit in, that I might come back and no one will recognize me. I know you will. But I really worry that everyone else won't. Especially because I left for school. Especially because I am writing all of our secrets.

Some nights, when the air is crisp and the sun is just touching down, I stand out on the bridge near my house and look down on the river and imagine I am home. The smell is different but there is a hint of something there that is the same, maybe all rivers have that ancient and dirty smell about them. I think about Pony and his being gone. I think about you and Mom and the old house. I spend a lot of time in my head.

Anyhow, Ohio is not the same. Which seems obvious, but then too, it is changing me and maybe I am not the same or will not be the same. Late at night, when I am trying to sleep, I list off all the places I miss from back home, all the things that I do not want to forget. You should come here. I'd like that. You're welcome anytime.

Jon

THE WAR AT HOME

I can tell Joe is looking to hit someone. He keeps bumping up against me, talking to the guy next to us a few stools over. We're at a bar along the river, a place called McGregor's, a place we only go when one or more of us has a good amount of money to spend. I hear Joe say, "I'm a fucking Marine motherfucker," see him take a drink from his pint. "I'll fucking kill you."

My brother is talking to Joe. "Calm down man," he says. "What did the guy do?" But it's clear the guy didn't do anything. "Let's go out and have a smoke," my brother says.

While they're outside Ralph and I explain it away: Just got back from a second tour in Iraq. All fucked up man. Doesn't mean anything by it.

We don't linger on Joe long. We distract the guy with sports. He's a Cubs fan, like Ralph, and they have that misery to share. But mostly we move off the subject, our friend, because we have no clue what's "wrong" with him and it's not so much him we're ashamed of as our own inability to describe things or make sense of them. We have no clue what our friend is going through, and, though it shames us to say it, we're comfortable not talking about it.

Outside Joe takes a swing at my brother, which isn't a safe thing to do, being that my brother is five inches taller, ninety pounds heavier. Joe misses and falls. He lies in the parking lot, cigarette dangling from his mouth, Atlanta Braves hat clinging to his shaved head. He starts crying, his pint glass a splash of shards stretching a few feet in front of him.

When Jeff comes inside again he is alone. The details of the conversation, cloudy. The war. Dead buddies. The kind of things we all imagine a vet might say but something Ralph and I don't have the stomach to go outside and witness ourselves.

"He'll be fine," Jeff says. "He just wanted some air and some time alone." Jeff refills his pint. "I'll go check on him in a minute."

I am thinking, when my brother comes back and reports the situation to us, about violence and how it has changed my friend. Or maybe, more accurately, I think it is something closer to love. How he loved the men in his company and how it broke his heart to watch them die. How it made him feel a deep and unshakeable guilt, being happy, if only for a second, that it was them and not him.

Of course I am guessing at this. I would never ask Joe the sorts of questions that could give me answers. And Joe will never say it, not like I have. He is a Marine. He is my friend, and we do not talk like that, not to one another. These are the types of things that we say to women we love, or it might be something Joe would only say to another Marine. There are things my friend will never say to me.

———

I remember another night when Joe beat a man bloody in The Ale House parking lot. I am thinking of all that love and all that hate and all those other things that are working through him as he pounds another man's face into the pavement.

It is a mess, this other man's body and Joe standing over him, people watching from the windows because it is snowing out and it is safer inside, but it doesn't last long.

As soon as it's clear it's over Joe reaches his hand down, and for a second, if I'd just gotten to the window, it might look like one friend helping another up. Joe pulls the man to his feet, wraps his arm around his neck, and carries him into the bar, where a group of us wait. We finish off our beers, getting a full glass for Joe's new friend. We drive the guy home. When we get there, Joe comes around the car, helps the guy out, bears the weight of the body as they limp together to the front door.

Later that night, after the beating, my brother and I return to the bar to clear things up with the bartender, who is always good to us. We want to make amends for Joe's actions. We want to make sure he'll be allowed back.

There we meet our friend Kim who is having a drink at the bar. Our friend wasn't there when the fight happened and so the bartender is filling her in. When he is done he turns to my brother and me and says, "Why would you guys want someone like that in your life?"

Before I can say anything Kim cuts in. "I think they just want to love him, even though they know he can't or won't be what they hope."

When we come out of McGregor's to end the night we can't find Joe. Ralph and I start calling out his name. Our voices echo off the river. We walk around the whole of the parking lot, back behind the dumpsters. He is gone.

"Don't worry," my brother says. "He probably started walking." Which is to say that Joe gets it in his mind sometimes, like he gets it in his mind to fight, that he should up and walk off.

"Where would he be walking to?" Ralph asks, a little drunk.

"Home," my brother says, which I find somehow comforting. We get in the car.

"It's six miles," Ralph says. "What the fuck is he thinking."

"He isn't," I say, pulling out of the parking lot.

We get a mile down the road, heading up a hill, when my brother spots Joe. It is cold out and Joe is only wearing a t-shirt and jeans and his baseball cap. His arms are tucked into his sleeves. He is visibly shivering.

"There he is," my brother says.

I pull over. My brother gets out. Joe and Jeff yell at one anther on the side of the road. My brother points to the car telling Joe to get in. He says other things about it being cold and something about why not take a ride. He goes back and forth between commanding and pleading. It feels like a long time. But the only thing I remember, even now, is Joe saying, "I'm fine man," saying "I just want to go home."

THIS ROOM AND EVERYTHING IN IT

Jeff is lounging in someone else's pool again. He is stripped down to his boxers, his arms outstretched over the tiled sides, cooling off in the August heat. He sings to himself. The rest of his clothes are a block over, sitting in his truck. His singing is too loud. He lounges there as if it were his own pool. He's been coming to this house for a few weeks now on his nights off, after drinking at Six Pockets. He couldn't resist cannon balling into the pool, hoping the loud splash wouldn't wake the homeowner, and now he's relaxing, singing, sobering up.

The bedroom light comes on. Jeff looks over his right shoulder toward the second floor, and only after he gets out toward the middle of the pool does he stop singing. The backyard is dark, the door about twenty feet from the edge of the inground pool. He waits for the kitchen light to flip on, not panicked or nervous but patient, to see if the homeowner will come out. Jeff is treading water, his arms making smooth circles. His head is back and his feet are floating up as if he were lying on the surface. He is only a bit worried about this, hoping that the pool and backyard lights stay off so he isn't caught there like some dead fish floating just beneath the water. He imagines the awkwardness of getting out all wet and being yelled at or threatened or the shock on their faces, all of it embarrassing if not a touch hilarious.

The kitchen light comes on and the female homeowner, a wife, a mother maybe, looks out into the backyard. She scans the property though it is unlikely in the dark that she can see much. Jeff looks back at her thinking he can float here forever if need be, though it will be morning before much longer. The woman turns to go back upstairs but suddenly decides to look out the back door. The lights flip on before she opens it. Jeff floats over toward the edge of the pool, and all he can think as the woman opens the back door is how hot it is and how good this feels.

He dips himself low in the water, his eyes peering over the edge. The woman is at the door now, and all the lights come on in the pool. Jeff slips beneath the surface. He goes down toward the bottom feeling the slippery sides and then the floor as he maneuvers back to the far side of the pool so he can see in the direction of the yard and watch for the woman's shadow. Nothing moves except the water all around him and he can hear the filter humming. He feels like he is frozen in a giant cube of ice. The light reflecting off the walls reveals every imperfection.

Jeff's room is a mecca, a place where any boy or even man would go to hide out. He has a new plasma screen TV, a Playstation 3, leather furniture. "Things are going to change," his father says over and over again. "Your friends are growing up, moving out, and you, all you have are this room and the things in it." It is constant, the advice, the pep talks. Jeff is twenty-five, lives in his sixty-two year old mother's apartment. He barely makes enough money in a month to cover his truck payment and beer money. What if his mother dies in her sleep? What if both his parents were gone, would his brother save him, help him get on his feet? Or, will he ever make it on his own? His brother lives in Columbus now with his girlfriend. This summer, he's told Jeff, is his last one in Rochester. Ralph, Jeff's best friend, has a house, just got tenured, is about to get married. Even if Jeff hadn't spent his money on new toys, the TV, the truck, where would he be? He'd be one more lonley bachelor without anything to offer. What if, he thinks, all he has are his things? He imagines the whole room submerged in water. He sits on his couch, the stereo and speakers sinking, and he thinks about how hard it is to hear anything underwater.

When he was a kid, like so many other kids, he trained for the day he'd need to hold his breath. Jeff and his brother would time each other and sometimes they would go under at opposite ends of the pool and shout things to one another and then they'd resurface and guess what the other had said. When they were underwater they could say anything, swear at one another or admit to liking some girl that they were both friends with. It didn't matter that the message rarely made it, and somedays Jeff would wish that he didn't have to come up.

THE CANCELLED LIFE

"This city was meant to be photographed," our tour guide tells us. "A hundred years after the founding of Kodak and the rise of photography as an art and Rochester is still the center of the world for film." I expect, on this tour, that we will not hear about layoffs or the digital age or the buildings Kodak is leveling to save money on taxes. In the slide show we watch there are pictures of all the important landmarks: the brewery, the Erie Canal, both the upper and lower falls. The documentation is meticulous. "You know," our tour guide, says, "the future happened here."

My father calls me on a Tuesday and says that they are razing some of the Kodak buildings on Friday and would I like to come watch with him. He is excited by the prospect of the explosion and the precision with which they will take the building down. A few seconds and it is over and all that's left is a pile, like snow plowed into the corner of a parking lot.

Photographers know no building will stand forever.

In a separate room designed to look like the future there are computers showing a history of the Kodak camera over the ages. It is set up like a peep show, wedding the old and the new, feeding coins, which are set alongside the computers in a basket, into a slot so the film will play. On screen, pictures of the first Kodak cameras appear and then decade-by-decade the film slides forward. Every other decade the machine requests another coin.

I am fascinated by the equipment. In one slide there is the first Kodak camera and in the next a disposable and even further down the line the digital equipment of today. Watching these screens gives the impression that with every passing year, with every new turn, Kodak has been cutting edge, has never fallen behind the curve.

I am led to believe that the future is happening here, now.

Kodak has factories along the river, liquid pouring from them and into the water below. In the summer, boaters pass the factories, and signs warn, "Eat No More Than Two Fish Per Season."

When we were little our father would dress us up, my brother and me, and take pictures of us. We would wear our baseball equipment or cowboy hats or glasses with big rubber noses attached to them. My father would work for hours on the lighting before he'd pose us. Like my GI Joe's, I liked to think. We might be holding up our fists or pointing a cap gun at the camera. From the basement where we'd wait, toys spread all around us, we could hear our father; "Damn it, that's not right," or "I wonder if I moved this here?" Before the advent of the disposable camera, and then digital, photography was real work.

There are a group of photographers there on Friday when they bring those dormant buildings down. They have been there for hours, maybe since yesterday, I suspect, setting their equipment at the right angles, working on exposure and how they expect the morning to frame their shots.

My mother remembers certain things about this city. She remembers Midtown and going there near Christmas with her roommates and watching the monorail circle the Christmas display and Santa Claus who sat high up on a fake mountain listening to kids and their wish lists. My mother, when we are kids, tells us about this every Christmas because it is gone now, one of those wonders that disappears from your life. She says that it was something to see, that building and all the lights and all the people. "Nothing like it is now," she says, staring out the kitchen window, "a kind of abandoned version of what I remember."

The whole city looks to the sky as a cloud rises and hovers. The news reports: "Nothing Left But Rubble."

Before I leave the room with the coins my father makes me watch it a second time. He points out the old cameras he used when he was taking courses at the state university in Brockport and before that the camera he used to take pictures of his buddies when he was in Vietnam. After the cameras he knows best, my father does not put another coin in the machine. He walks away without saying a word. He wants nothing to do with the world and its change.

At the senior ball, the school hands out a pint glass and a disposable Kodak camera. This, to me, is a mixed message because prior to prom we signed forms that promised we would not drink. Still, the camera seems useful. *How will you remember this night?* the packaging asks.

I take pictures of girls I have had a crush on since grade school and some of my favorite teachers dancing.

But I never develop the roll.

There are pictures of my brother and me with our mother holding us, in the hospital or even later at home, hundreds of them. About them there is no sense of order. It feels, looking at them, as if they were shot rapidly and without the same concern for lighting and angle that my father showed when he dressed us up. Instead it feels like our parents were collecting as much proof as they can, like my brother and I might not even be real.

In September Kodak announces that it will be cutting 900 jobs. The stock plummets. It looks like a person flung from a building, falling straight down. One wonders if there is a bottom, a place where it will sort of "splat." This is broadcast at noon, and so by five, when people are going home, rush hour, they cut through the center of the city, which is mostly Kodak, to see if there is some sort of visible change in the buildings or the streets.

On Main Street, 900 people stand outside the Kodak tower. It seems ironic now that only three letters light up. K-O-D... As if the other two lights were powered by those 900 bodies now standing in the street. Traffic is backed up, moving very slowly, like a long funeral precession winding its way through the center of the city. No one can decide what to make of it. Or everyone feels something must be made of it, those workers holding their briefcases and lunch pails.

What are they waiting for?

I remember a commercial in the 80s that showed a cartoon camera running around the city and snapping off pictures. Then he'd take us back to a Kodak factory and show us how the film was made and how cameras were assembled. "Kodak," he said, "It's where the magic happens."

I look for it, during the tour, to see if it is how I remembered it. But I cannot find it.

There is more news of layoffs today. This time Xerox, who once had its national headquarters in Rochester. When they put that logo up on the screen, that white sheet of paper with the red X, it almost looks like someone waving a white flag of surrender.

On our tour there is a lot of talk about George Eastman, Kodak's founder. We see a lot of his original photographs of the city. He is especially fascinated by the natural construction of it; the river, the waterfalls, the power.

In one of his diaries he writes: *The potential for growth and prosperity in the city of Rochester is apparent just by looking at the power of the Genesee River.*

My childhood home was in permanent shade. The Kodak buildings towered over it. We would, as kids, ride our bikes by men and women in business attire who were going on their lunch breaks or headed out for drinks after twelve-hour days. The neighborhood swelled with diners and donut shops and sports bars. Every now and then we'd work up the courage to ride to the end of the Kodak complex and take turns peeping in through the cracks in the tinted windows outside *The Mirage Palace*. We all came to believe that this was one of those benefits our parents talked about when they talked about Kodak and its incentives packages.

My father was a janitor so my family never directly benefited from the holiday bonuses that the "big" companies like Kodak, Xerox, and Bausch & Lomb, gave. Still, he did get his own little bonus and he'd spilt it up evenly, one hundred dollars for my mother, my brother, and me.

The news announced each year when the big bonuses had been given out, and they sent camera crews to cover the rush at the local malls. One Christmas, my family was there when the newscasters descended on Marketplace Mall. My father stood with a shit eating grin, his wife and boys at his side. At the time, he had a gold cap on his front tooth and my friends called him snaggletooth. A man from news channel 10 was interviewing my father about the holidays and how he was going to spend his Christmas bonus. It was clear he thought my father worked for Kodak or one of the other bigger employers. Still, the guy never asked outright and my father never let on that the man's assumption was wrong.

"My family gets whatever they want," my father said.

"Anything," the newscaster replied, a look of sheer awe on his face.

"Anything," my father said, pulling us in close so the camera could capture all of us smiling.

My father walked around the mall for the rest of that night with his chest puffed out and a goofy grin on his face. He seemed happy, like he might after watching the Buffalo Bills win a football game or after drinking a twelve-pack with my uncle Steve. He walked around the mall like he was a king.

It is still believed today, by many cultures, that a photograph is capable of stealing one's soul. It's one of the reasons in photographs of Native American's why they sit so stiff backed, defiant. Because they know that this is not a keepsake, but another form of robbery.

Many cultures accept the faulty nature of memory. They know even the photograph only gets it halfway right. They believe there is only one way to bring the dead back to life, story.

On the tour we stop often to watch short films. There is one, shot on Kodak reels, about the old trolley system. In it the trolley flies down city streets, stopping to let people on and off. The city is alive, people going in and out of buildings, boarding and exiting the trolley. Alongside it, horses pull carts full of Genesee beer and flour. The city, in this film, seems very much like it is on the rise. I am, even for a second, kind of proud of this city, am energized by the idea of our newness and successes. The film plays for ten minutes and never mentions that the trolley only survived for a few years, that it was built over the aqueduct where the canal once ran, another technology that collapsed in its own short time.

The old aqueduct, which served as a tunnel for the trolley, is abandoned now. It cuts right through the center of downtown and serves as a bridge crossing the Genesee right before the highest of the three famous waterfalls. Sam Patch jumped from a spot fifty yards from here when he attempted his second and fatal jump from the falls. Now it is a shelter for the homeless during the winter months.

The aqueduct was originally built as an offshoot of the canal, so there are secondary channels for barges, docking and storage areas for resupply and product transfer. When you enter it from Main Street there are a set of stairs that disappear into the belly of the old library building, where they house local history now. The main collection is across the street in a new building. There is a door that goes into the basement of the old library; legend has it that the city's founders would retreat here were the city under attack, escaping through the library into the belly of the city and through the canal out onto lake Ontario. Beyond that and into the main channel, everything is covered in graffiti. My friends and I came here and wrote our names on the wall in black spray paint. But there are also colorful murals and portraits done by very talented taggers, who have recreated the canal, or a fistfight, or a picture of a loved one who is dead. Groups of homeless men congregate in the old storerooms and docks. Their possessions line the walls and are sprawled out in front of them in small piles. They are safe here, underground, away from the cold and snow of winter in Upstate New York.

It is strange to think of a group of citizens hidden beneath the ground, with their own rules and kind of government.

During the summer the tunnels will be abandoned for life above ground, every corner downtown crowded with shopping carts full of clothes and bottles and other keepsakes. Their homes in the aqueduct go largely vacant for the whole of the warm weather months.

My mother remembers how Eastman Theater swelled to capacity on Saturday nights, how people would buy tickets months in advance to go, to be a part of what was happening there. The only time I was there was for my high school graduation, the pristine halls and ceilings muted by the joking of eighteen-year-old boys and the cries of eighteen-year-old girls. Most of the time we were cramped in the seats, five hundred of us waiting to walk the stage and get our pictures taken with the principal. And all I really remember is the guys around me talking about doing stupid things as they walked across the stage.

Ten years after my graduation and the theater is still there but something about it seems less alluring. Now there are bars and coffee shops all around it. Like the city has shed it, old skin, and a new set of minor attractions have surpassed it.

When my friend, who works for Kodak, talks about his job, he says that every six months you can expect to be next. It is like waiting with your neck in the noose, but without knowing when they are going to kick the floor out from under you. There are five months of safety and then a month of breath holding and then you start all over again. "But, fuck," he says. "At least I have work, for now." Which has become our motto, our kind of catch phrase for how the city is. And no one is surprised when one business or another closes, by the news of new layoffs or cutbacks.

They dismantle the buildings on Ridge Road one piece at a time. There are too many businesses on the other side of the street, most of them opened when Kodak was still going strong and most of them dying with it. They take down the buildings this way because they can't blast them down here, like they did on Lake Ave., because they'd have to close six lanes of traffic. Instead, for three months we watch them pull it down. Brick by brick. The dust from drywall and broken light bulbs floating over traffic. And then one day we drive by and there is nothing left but a field of freshly planted grass.

My father confronts the tour guide. "What about the future?" he asks. Everyone on the tour freezes. For the first time our tour guide appears stumped. I sense, in my father, a certain amount of regret. After all, the guide is just a high school kid. What does he know about the past or the future? What do we expect him to reveal to us except for the things he's memorized from the script?

During the winter, everything is caked in ice and the city looks like it lives in suspension.

My father wants to know why I write about the city. He shows me pictures of my grandfather working on the railroad, coal dust smeared on his uniform and on his face. During my father's childhood my grandfather was gone for months at a time. He lived in mobile camps and was a cook. Late in his career, when the trains began fading away, my grandfather would be home for months on end. My father claims his father was restless, would often go for long walks, lasting hours, or chop wood until the sun went down, just to simulate the work that was slowly drying up. The man could hardly sit through a whole meal.

"That's work," my father says.

Kodak holds camps in the summer where kids can come and learn how to photograph the cityscape. Some of the pictures from the last summer camp are on display at the end of our tour. They start at the lake and work their way into the city, past the zoo where a new section has been built for the polar bears, and then down river to the Kodak Industrial Park where they are taking down buildings. I see pictures outside the Gazette Newspaper Building, of the War Memorial across the street. And then there are hundreds of shots of the upper falls, of the new buildings, bars and nightclubs and art galleries, going up there. Across the river, spray-painted on one of the brewery outbuildings, in sloppy handwriting, are the words Impeach Duffy, the current mayor. This one seems to have slipped through the censors because there are other pictures, obvious things, the Kodak building and the Hyatt and Mark's Texas Hots, but nothing that suggests strife. They are of the kind of places people think of when they think of downtown.

The interesting thing about the shots is not what is or is not in them. Instead, when I flip one over I see that they are printed on Fuji film. I don't ask just then but later phone the camp and ask why Kodak would let them do this. "Actually," the head counselor says, "Kodak donates money and we buy the cameras."

"Why Fuji?" I ask. "Doesn't that seem a bit disloyal?"

He pauses for a second. I feel like I might be the first person to have called and asked about this. He clears his throat. "It happens," he says, "that that summer Fuji was cheaper."

All I see are the flashbulbs, the shadows in the negatives, the streaks of light of bodies in motion. This is how the city will die. Smiling, frozen in anticipation of one final photograph. This is our way. To grit our teeth and bare it, the way we do when winter wind comes off the lake. The buildings falling around us like music accompanying the closing credits.

I can hear the building fall that Friday when they take it down. We watch from the balcony of my father's apartment, twenty-one floors from the ground. I close my eyes and imagine it. I know I will be able to watch the slow motion replay on the news that night. I want to hear it collapse.

I wait for my father's voice. "Jesus," he says. And then the voices of the other people who live in the complex, many of them Kodak retirees who have just gotten word that a part of their healthcare is being cut. I hear the man behind me say, "Serves those fuckers right."

The dust is still rising when I open my eyes. It is streaming out over the roads that have been closed for today's demolition. The construction workers around the site have their arms raised, blocking out the sun, taking in the full effect of their work. It will be hours before everything settles into a neat pile.

My father has been taking pictures of this city for nearly 30 years. He has pictures of places that I would never know of if not for his photographs. "It's changed a lot," he says, as we leaf through one of his photo albums. Often, after we look through his photographs, we go out to a diner. On the way I try to image the city the way it looks in my father's pictures, I try to imagine what George Eastman saw when he first came here. As we drive through the city, large gaps where the old buildings once stood, my father points and calls out the names of the places that are missing, the names of places from the past.

THE BRIGHT NIGHT EFFECT

Rochester is snowed in. Like the rest of New York and all the cities laid down along the lake. The city is under siege. There is gray in the sky and smoke funneling from Kodak. The lake threatens to wash away the summer homes of people who do not stay to brave the winter but anxiously watch the weather report. The city council has been gassing up the plows since August in preparation. Grade schoolers still walk to school, tunneling through six-foot tall snowdrifts and arriving late after epic snowball wars. The parking lots conquered and reconquered with the removal and arrival of fresh snow. Rush hour traffic and holiday travel go unaffected except for the out-of-towners who are going too slow.

The bars along the river have closed their doors until April and handed out what was left of the summer stock. We're moving into the city, moving closer to one another. The warmth of 100,000 people melts the snow on Saturday nights. But we don't retreat into our homes. There is ice fishing and snowmobiling and games of hockey to be played on the frozen canal. Everywhere you go you hear whispers: *hypothermia, through the ice.* Children are not praying for snow days because they know there is never enough, that more snow only means longer walks and salt stained pants. The hills of salt at the town hall become smaller as the snow piles higher, as shopping carts from Wegman's grocery become mangled and lost, as the inevitable child goes missing, a snow fort caved in.

On *R News* Yolanda Vega is calling out the numbers for the New York "Take 5" and we are on the edge of our seats because my mother always buys a ticket and because we are mesmerized by Yolanda's voice. When she calls out her name, "Hello New York, this is Yo-LAN-dah VAY-ga," drawing it out, it almost makes it all right that we will never win. We love Yolanda. We love the snow. They are constant. They are here to stay. Or they will return again. There will be no layoffs, no jobs shipped to other cities never to return.

After the break, the news reports that sales are down at local retail outlets, and they explore the connection between that and decreases in Kodak bonuses and layoffs at Delphi and cutbacks at Xerox. It is no wonder everyone in this town is holding a lottery ticket. The weatherman comes on with spectacular photos of the city covered in snow, and he describes some kind of effect with the light. There is always something new to learn about snow and winter weather. My friends and I, though we are too old and do not have the right winter gear, find old sleds in our garages and go out into the snow with beer and a camera. We have forgotten flashlights but the weatherman, for once, was right. The light from the city is bouncing off the clouds and it is bouncing back off the snow and it is almost like the sun is just now rising, even though it's well past midnight. All at once the world feels beautiful, more than I can say. From the top of the hill where we stand, in one of those silent moments that comes when the world appears covered in snow, every inch of the city is burning.

THE INS AND OUTS OF SCIENCE

I was twelve the summer a boy in my neighborhood drowned. He was five and lived around the corner from me and he died on his birthday. I played soccer with his brother and the news of his death spread down the sidelines from parent to parent like a game of telephone. A Vietnam veteran and a man of few words, my father said to my brother and me, "You should never swim alone," as if death were something one could, with caution, indefinitely prevent. My mother was more affectionate. Having known the boy, having been to all our soccer games that summer, she held us tighter that week, paid closer attention when we were outside, cheered louder from her seat on the sidelines of the soccer field.

I was, like my friends, at twelve, taken with death. I spent hours fighting wars in our sandbox with my G.I. Joes, killing off my least favorite and using broken soldiers for spare parts during explosions. My friends and I learned to fake our deaths: throwing our bodies to the ground and violently flailing during cap gun fights, or dodging water balloons as if they were hand grenades during military style games of capture the flag. We perfected the art of dying. War was a game that created heroes—at least we believed it could—and death, during games like these, was something a five-minute time out, a new T-shirt, or the start of a new game could fix. In the movies we watched, heroes reigned: saving pretty girls in distress, defeating armies, conquering cities with swords and crossbows. Fear, danger, death, all became obsolete elements in the lives our heroes lived.

But here was death before me, near me. Though the boy who drowned hadn't been my age, I felt more connected to him than I had any aunt or uncle I'd lost. But his drowning didn't have the same affect on my friends. He had snuck out to the pool, during a lull in the birthday party, and tried to fill the water gun he'd gotten while the other kids played in the air-conditioned house and parents cleaned up leftover cake. I saw his five-year-old body in my dreams that summer, floating in the pool one street from my house.

I had seen dead bodies before. When I was four my grandfather passed away, and at the funeral I stuck my hand in his coffin thinking he was asleep. When I was nine my aunt died, and all I could imagine as we drove to her house was how she'd taught my brother and me to play UNO, how, for as long as we'd known her, she'd been in a wheelchair or in a bed with machines around her. What I remembered most was how "juiceless" the bodies looked. How deflated. They looked to me like cartoon characters crushed by construction equipment, waiting to inflate again.

Still, I couldn't imagine the boy the way I'd seen other dead bodies. In my dreams, he always looked alive, his body plump and full despite his motionless limbs. My mother was a nurse in the emergency room and I became fascinated by the idea of her seeing people just before their deaths. I'd ask her over and over again what death was like, but she'd shrug me off, tell me that it was nothing for me to worry about.

That summer I wondered what drowning felt like. I wondered how long it took before the body finally gave up, and I really wanted to know if the boy had floated or sunk. I'd go underwater and hold my breath and try to keep myself from surfacing but my lungs always burned and something inside always forced me up. I could see his parents finding him in their pool, dead. And I could hear his mother's screams, something different than the cheering she'd done at the soccer fields, something more desperate. What illuminated my dreams about the boy's death was how sudden it was, how unpredictable.

My cousin, around the same time, was fighting cancer, his twenty-six-year-old body slowly decaying and rebuilding and decaying again. For years he was in and out of cancer wards and when we'd visit him, my mother and my brother and I, we'd have to wear masks to protect him from us. What fascinated me about these visits was how we talked about progress, how every step without a walker, every increased white blood cell count, every solid meal consumed was cause for celebration, as if death had reduced us to cheering for all the things that came easily to the rest of us. But even when he wasn't walking, or his count was down, there was the belief that he could beat death, that if we washed our hands before we went in, if we wore masks, if we avoided visiting when we were sick, that all his bad luck would turn good.

My father felt he could make his own luck when it came to death. He relied on labels that read disinfectant, anti-bacterial, antiseptic. He scrubbed the toilet seats, cleaned the counters, and washed his hands with a ferocity that germs, he believed, could not defeat. When a toothbrush was left on a counter, he yelled out into the hallways, imagining everyone was listening, about putting things in their appropriate and uncontaminated place. His hypochondria drove him, hours consumed making sure he'd taken the correct vitamins, setting appointments with doctors, feeling under his arm and around his neck for lumps. The refrigerator door rattled like a sack of marbles whenever I opened it, vitamin bottles clanking together. My brother and I mocked him whenever our mother made steak for dinner because he microwaved his piece and didn't sit down with us until we were almost done. Sometimes the meat looked like roadkill, steam rising off it in large waves, the fat around the edges crispy and shriveled. I couldn't imagine how he ate it but if we asked he'd talk about mad cow or other diseases borne in undercooked meat, all the while heaping on salt like it was a cure.

The summer of the drowning I went swimming almost every day at my best friend, Ralph's, house. We spent hours shallow diving in the five-foot deep pool, playing Marco Polo with the solar cover on so you'd have to burst through it to get air, tightrope walking the rails of the pool when we were "fish out of water." My friends were fearless, setting up ramps and launching their bikes into the pool, building platforms to dive from, screaming until their voices were hoarse and they spoke with whispers. We thought that bigger stunts would mean bigger fun, would be a way of proving who was a "pussy" and who was not. My buddy's mother always yelled at us. A retired Dean, she had no patience for boys, and her son had become a failed product of that impatience. "Get down from there," she'd yell. "You're going to break your neck!"

When school started I went to the library and did research on drowning. Our swimming days, for the next eight months, were over, but the boy who'd died that summer was still with me and I needed to know what it looked like. At first glance I was taken with statistics. I read how drowning is one of the leading causes of death for boys under fourteen, how 6,500 people drown in the United States every year, how it is estimated that ten percent of all children ages 5 and under "experienced a situation with a high risk of drowning." What was better were their explanations of situations. It made me, though I felt like I shouldn't, want to laugh. "PCP users frequently lose their sense of direction as well, and drowning is a major cause of death for them." Things like this had me laughing to myself all day in class. I imagined myself on an especially big sugar high, "Too much soda," my father might say, lurching toward a pool with no control over my body. I wanted to share my drowning facts with my mother and my cousin as we sat in his room later that night, but he was having an especially good day and I didn't want to chance ruining it. He'd gone the whole day without an oxygen mask and had colored with his son in their favorite coloring book.

But there was science—explaining the finality of it, the pain I felt in my lungs when I was making myself stay under water—keeping my curiosity alive. That burning, that need to reach the surface again is called *air hunger*, and I found out that it had less to do with oxygen than it did with carbon dioxide: "The urge to breathe is triggered by rising carbon dioxide levels in the blood rather than diminishing oxygen levels." And there were terms to learn: *asphyxia, hypoxia, brain damage, air hunger, suffocation, death.* The books I looked at had pictures, which appeared fake, of kids lying at the bottom of pools with their arms stretched out, their hair floating around like sea weed. Those books told me that it would take five to eight minutes for my body to go limp (unconscious), for brain damage to set in, for me to be dead.

At twelve I still had a disregard for this science. Because of my new found obsessions with death I found comfort in sledding down "suicide hill," walked without caution on thin ice, rode my bike without a helmet as if I were daring myself, placing myself against death. Science was what explained my cousin's evaporation; it was what allowed them to implant a shunt in his arm so they could run IV's without having to open a vein over and over again, it was his bald head, a head his three-year-old son had never seen with hair. Oxygen and carbon dioxide and white blood cells: I thought of these things as objects I could trade like baseball cards. The way I'd pick at scabs to watch them bleed, the way I'd rip off band-aids to show off new scars, the way my young body twisted and contorted while my friends and I wrestled in our front yards. There was something innocent and stupid about being a twelve-year-old boy, something science wouldn't allow.

I saw death everywhere. The winter after the boy drowned and before my cousin got really sick, six of us went to the woods to sled. Marching through the deep forest on a path cut by sledders, we threw snowballs at one another. We came to an opening, the foot of the hill we'd planned on sledding, and even before we saw the crowd we could hear the screams. A boy our age had veered off the path, run headlong into a tree and broken his neck.

That night, after my friends and I got home from sledding, we sat around the television and waited for a news report about that boy. "Do you think it will be on?" Ralph asked. "Of course it will, dumbass," my brother replied. We were all secretly concerned but we made light of it. "I bet it looked like this," Ralph said, playing out the scene as if he were headed for the tree. His feet faced forward, his head bent low, but always at the last second he'd spring from his imaginary sled, roll dangerously close to the tree, but elude it. "That tree would never have gotten me," he'd said.

Somewhere inside, I hated that boy. He'd ruined our day, closed down the hill, and what's more, unlike the boy from the summer, I could see that this kid was important to my friends, that his injuries and possible death scared them. We were all hoping he'd do to death what Ralph claimed he would have masterfully done if faced with that tree.

When we found out a few days later that the sledding kid was dead, we were dejected but only in the way a boy might be after losing a bet. It remained with us, but like all good gamblers, we laughed it off. We may have even talked about it, before we knew what had happened, like we were bookies taking in Vegas size money. "I bet ya he never walks again." "I bet the kid's already dead." When we finally heard the news, he was dead, we never mentioned that kid or that day again.

It was a winter day like this, a few weeks later, when I'd be at an aunt's house and find out my cousin Tommy had cancer again. My mother made it sound like it was nothing. Not that she didn't acknowledge the severity of it, but she explained to my brother and me that it was the same cancer Mario Lemieux, our favorite hockey player, had had and that he had overcome it. Mario Lemieux was going to be in the Hall of Fame. Mario Lemieux had won two Stanley Cups.

Tommy's son was walking since the last time I'd seen him and Tommy was bald now, having gone through his first round of chemo treatment. Still, he'd go into work the number of days required to get his health insurance, and when he thought I was getting out of line he'd yell, "Jonathan."

Most of that night at my aunt's is forgotten, pushed out by Christmas presents, turkey, the women at the kitchen table, the men in the basement watching football on TV. All I remember now is my cousin's face, how he gritted his teeth and looked over at me and said my name. I can see the light of some candles or the Christmas tree shining off his hairless head. I can see him smile when I say, "I'm going to cut my hair just like you."

Tommy, despite his sickness, was always asking me about my future even when I was growing increasingly less certain about his.

"How many girls are you dating these days?"

"How is hockey coming along, you going to be a pro soon?"

And he always made sure to heckle me, telling me how I was goofy like my father, reminding me: "With those glasses and that hair cut you look just like him."

Sometimes during visits we walked, my mother and me, with him, doing his daily lap around the desk in the center of the unit that held the nurses and the sinks and the masks. My mother was confident during these visits despite her knowledge as a nurse always being tested. One day, during our second lap, he asked, "What do you think about this bone marrow transplant, Aunt Joan?"

"It is definitely something worth considering. I think, with your brother donating, there is a good chance."

It was hope, this science, but in the ward, where one door had to close behind you before you could go through the next, where each patient had his or her own room sealed off from the world, science meant more to me than it would at school, when we were dissecting animals, when we were learning about genus and species.

What began to consume me more and more during that winter was science, what science thought it could determine and what it simply couldn't. For example, they could tell Tommy where his cancer was, they could tell him the exact number of white blood cells he had on any given day, but they could never explain why Taco Bell was the only solid food his body could keep down. I joked to myself that he was a circus act. My ads read: Not for the Faint of Heart: The only man in America who can eat Taco Bell every day and still look like a cancer patient. Come see the only man in America who can eat Taco Bell and not get sick. I wasn't trying to be cruel, and had I said these things to Tommy, he would have known what I meant. I knew we were both confused, those months before winter hit, about the ins and outs of science.

My father was a firm believer in medicine, trying to outguess his body, trying to remain three head colds or a terminal illness ahead. Medicine was a tool that promised my father his chance to elude death. And my friends and I, in our naive way, believed that our bodies would naturally do something akin to his miracle cures, his Icy Hot, his supplements that warded off injury and sickness. We based our knowledge on all our "near death" encounters—whatever that meant—and placed our bodies at the mercy of luck. We even considered, for some time, that we were invincible like our heroes; we truly thought that the lives we knew would stretch out before us like a long and endless road. But, what the summer and then the winter had shown me was how naïve we were to think this.

I saw—when we were sitting there with Tommy, him telling about a day or a week's worth of events—that medicine could be as confusing as those science textbooks, as uncertain and unpredictable as a five-year-old boy drowning in a pool on his birthday. Tommy's body was a medical mystery fluctuating over the course of five years like lines on a seismograph. Around it, in swimming pools and classrooms, at the dining room table, was my father burning hamburgers, was my mother calmly answering questions, were my friends and I flirting with death. It wasn't until the second bone marrow transplant, until his doctors found a hole in his esophagus that I stopped believing Tommy's disease was like one of my father's steaks, something that could be burnt away, that Tommy could be salted back to life.

———

All I could think about the day my cousin died was chocolate ice cream. On the ride home from the hospital, a memory I had from weeks earlier flashed through my head, a story Tommy had told me. He had, one day, had a craving for ice cream and in frustration pulled himself from his bed and made an attempt to flee. As he told it, I could see his feet gliding over the tile floor. I could picture him dragging those IV's behind him looking like a poorly conceived science project. I could hear his voice rising in irritation, telling the nurse, "I can go if I want to," sounding like it had that night at my aunt's when he was continually yelling my name. He told it with a smile, laughing at himself, and there was something in the telling that invited me to laugh along with him.

And now, being twenty-six myself, I've got ice cream on my mind and I want something more for him. As I imagine it this time, I'm cheering his escape. After he's made it through the doors and past the distracted nurse, there is nothing but a smooth elevator ride between him and the street. He stands there once he's reached the ground floor, his feet in slippers, his sweatpants loose around his waist, looking down both sides of the street before him. And he moves toward the end that looks most promising, trying to remember where his room would be, where he'd seen that grocery store from his window. As I imagine it, I see him weaving in and out of traffic, moving at a snail's pace, drawn on by a ferocity that I can measure only through the movement of his arms as they sweep past his legs. And they will find him, hours later, his back up against a cooler, empty containers at his feet, his face like a child's, covered in chocolate.

OTHER LIVES

I

You were eight the year your mother was murdered. He'd kill ten more prostitutes over the next two years before they'd find him, The Genesee River Killer. Your father, by the time I'd met you, had remarried. The year they caught that man, we were ten, playing in your basement when you told me. I'd been making a joke of it, the guy who'd killed prostitutes. His capture and confession were all over the news that year. I was saying how it was no wonder—with a name like Arthur Shawcross—he was a serial killer.

"My mother was his first victim," you said.

II

I lived a few blocks from you. Your father was jobless and your stepmother was a bank teller. My father was a janitor and my mother was a nurse. We were city boys, playing baseball without real bases and playing tackle football without equipment.

During the summer, we swam in your pool. Your new mother, who all your friends—myself included—thought was hot, always seemed agitated by us.

Again in your basement, you told me your father had been married five or six times, he'd had fifteen kids, and you didn't think, not for one second, that either of you would be here much longer.

You were right. By sixth grade, you were gone. I hung out with you only one time after that. We were fourteen and I spent the night at your father's apartment downtown. When I got there you told me he was in his bedroom with his girlfriend, and that the living room, which doubled as your bedroom, was where we'd be sleeping. We were bored and looking for trouble to occupy us.

So we drank. We wandered Rochester's streets, and you told me one day you'd be just like your daddy. "Just like him," you said.

We were still boys. We were getting drunk. I didn't think much about what that meant. I only knew that when we got back from our walk the TV in his room was blaring, and you and I couldn't stop laughing, and my mother, when she found out we'd drank, never let me go back.

III

I was in my first year at college the last time I saw you. Home in Rochester for the summer, I'd heard from someone I'd worked with that your father had died of AIDS, that he had, in those years before your real mother had been killed, pimped her out for drug money so he could get high.

I walked into Schaller's, the burger joint on Ridge Road just a block down from where I worked. There you were. I was with a group of neighborhood friends, guys like me—most of them—who had gone off to college, who were home working summer jobs, who were here looking for food before late-night drinking. You were the same wild-eyed kid I'd spent that night with years before. The same curly haired kid whose pool I'd swam in summers ago.

But your eyes seemed glazed over like shiny marbles. And I didn't know what to say.

You stuck out your hand. "How are you?" you said.

I told you I'd gone to college, I was doing well. I didn't want to ask how you were. I'd known guys who'd worked at that burger joint. Most of them never planned on leaving home or doing anything other than drinking or snorting things with the money they'd made.

What I remember, about that night, was what my friend Ralph said when I got to the table: "You didn't expect that, did you?" But I did, and when you mentioned your girl, the second baby on the way, when you said how hard it was, working to feed babies and stay sober, I didn't have it in me to ask about your stepmother or your old house or even your father.

It wasn't the questions I didn't ask, and it wasn't the guilty silence that followed. When I let out that nervous laugh, that must have been the part that hurt the most.

IN A TOWN THAT DREAMS ONLY OF SNOW

We go there, once a year, my brother, father, and I. The same people go every year. And like most bars, the same few people are there every night. It is a holdover, the type of place that seems to have been there forever. Four Brothers is a Ukrainian bar, from when the neighborhood was mostly Eastern European, in a section of Rochester that is mostly black today. The owner, John, has been running the bar for twenty years and took over from his father. John knows everyone's name, black, Ukrainian, or otherwise. John keeps the bar open Christmas Eve and Christmas. He is a guard against loneliness.

We go to see Dave. Uncle Dave, he insists. Uncle Dave is always there. He is rumored to be a fortuneteller, a gypsy, and some say he never really returned from Vietnam but came home, in his mind, for a short leave. I listen close when he speaks because I believe, even now at twenty-six, that Dave has some answer for me, that he can tell me something about the future and what it holds for my brother, my father and me.

My father goes to the bar on Christmas Eve. He goes without us. While we have dinner with our mother, he goes, to have the free chicken dinner John gives to any customer who buys a beer that night. It's a ritual, this going out on Christmas, this drinking, this bonding of fathers and sons and has been since our father left (four years ago) or—to be fair—was thrown out by our mother. We don't ask about his leaving and neither our mother nor our father talks about it.

This year we start at my father's new apartment, which he has invited us over to see. Now that he is collecting Social Security and receiving a small pension he has moved out of the tiny room he kept at the syrup factory and into a subsidized high-rise for people in their sixties. He lives on the twenty-second floor of a twenty-three-floor building. We stare out the bedroom window and examine the expressway and the river. My father says it is a beautiful view, all the lights and traffic and the water, once it gets dark, like it is now.

It is cold outside and the lake is dumping snow on the city in response, I imagine, to people's prayers for a white Christmas. I can feel a draft from the old bay window we stand in front of.

The smell of urine seeps in from the hallway and other apartments.

I hear the TV in the living room, which my father has just purchased and has set on the box it came in. He has almost no furniture. Doesn't even have a bed. He sleeps on a blue mat, which he put on top of an old folded out futon frame. Two of the chairs at his kitchen table are lawn chairs he took from my mother's patio when he came one night to watch a hockey game while she was out.

My brother stands with his arms folded, enjoying the view, though he is quiet about it. He and my father, when I step back, look like a photograph, a representation of fathers and sons. They stand looking out, one on either end of the window, speechless.

Staring out the same window, knowing soon that we will go to Four Brothers, knowing we will go to see Dave, I wonder if my father will be okay, if he really enjoys this view, I wonder how he feels about me, his oldest son, who has left Rochester for Ohio.

It is safe to assume that Dave will say nothing important this year, as he is usually without the information I most want. Still, I will listen.

My father has his shirt off, which makes me wonder if he is cold. And even with a shirt on and without glasses, I see so much of my father in my brother.

The coffee pot is sucking up the last of the water my father has put in it. I am sure it is a full pot. He always makes too much.

It feels like a long time, their standing there and my watching and I even begin to wonder what it might look like to a stranger standing even further behind me. How these three men, who look so much alike with their height and short hair, my father and me with glasses on, fit together like pieces of a collage. I don't know if they can hear it, but our standing here like this is the kind of conversation the three of us have all the time.

The news is not good tonight. The news here, like most everywhere, is never good.

My father insists upon watching it before we go out.

From the 22nd floor the news sounds different, less important or less impending. I am not sure I like it more but I am more comfortable with it.

My father does not, throughout the whole of the broadcast, comment on the stories or turn them into an argument or lecture to my brother and me. This is different.

Perhaps this is a good place, a good distance from the ground for the three of us.

II. At the Table Having Coffee Before Four Brothers

My father's hands remind me of the summer and working construction and how bloody and dried out a man's hands can look after that kind of work. He has a pocket of blood under his thumbnail, but I do not ask him about it. We are sitting in his kitchen/living room on my mother's lawn chairs drinking coffee, staring at the television and watching the end of the news.

The forecast calls for more snow.

I am thinking, sitting in this mostly unfurnished apartment with the smell of urine seeping in from the hall, of my father's best friend Harold who lived in this building and who died a few summers ago. I remember how we went to Harold's apartment, only that one time, my brother and me with our father, and took his things because he left them all (what little there was) to my father. I can see us sitting there putting our hands on his things. I am fingering the backs of books deciding which to take and which to leave. My father is going through the fridge for food and my brother is unhooking the speakers attached to Harold's stereo.

Harold lived on the other side of the building with a better view of the river. I see the river, see something like that scene in my father's room, the three of us, my brother and father and me, standing at the window and looking down into the river. We talked about how a man might kill himself jumping from that height. Or maybe we talked about how it was for Harold living there with that view. Harold's room smelled like piss because his cancer had immobilized him. He was forced to pee in jars or sometimes he went right in his bed.

Back in the kitchen at my father's table we talk a bit about the Christmas cards taped to his otherwise barren walls. It is interesting to see who has sent a card to both my mother and father, where their lives still intersect. We talk about this weather and who is going to drive to Four Brothers and who is going to stay sober enough to get us all home.

This coffee and small talk are how we spend every Christmas before we go to Four Brothers to meet Uncle Dave and learn something about our lives. My brother and I will tell everyone about Uncle Dave, will analyze for days what he has said and what he hasn't. We imagine his words are a sermon meant only for us. I want Uncle Dave added to a list of strange people and places in the state. No one will take him seriously, I suppose. Maybe for me that is the magic of it.

My brother puts more sugar in his coffee after every sip, stirs with his finger, and licks the finger clean of his sugary concoction. I don't tell either of them how much they look alike, my brother and father, how I feel when I am sitting between them like I am sitting with two ghosts born of the same man.

I will leave and then come back to visit and something about me or about the way people see me will change. One night after drinking with my brother he will say to me, because he is drunk and frustrated, "Some of the guys don't like you anymore." This means that I better watch myself, that I am an outsider now, not to the people I am close to, but to the people on the outskirts of our group.

But too, I hear it in my brother's voice when he has been drinking. "College boy," he says, and there is certain venom there, a kind of hate that is deep and old, something he might usually exercise through action. After all, I have left and the odds are good that I am not coming back. And I wear a tie when I teach. And I am writing, about this city, about the places we have gone and the things we have done. Perhaps what I am doing is breaking a kind of code.

III. We Have Ventured to the Roof

Other than snow there is wind to contend with once we are on the roof. The door was unlocked. My father checked a few nights ago and he insisted, after coffee, that we come here to get the full effect. There is ice and there is the dark itself, which we seem suddenly close to, and there is the river in full view. The water washing out to the lake, a turning, swirling mass of movement that will soon be frozen over, but only on top. Who knows what's still moving beneath. The sudden suspension of a body as it crashes through. Panic, and then nothing. My father, when we were kids, walked out on the ice and it caved in, swallowing him and the family dog. He was trying to show us how safe it was, how thick and conquered by the cold. We fished him out, my brother and I, his hands gripped tight around our arms. Water rushing around his body and beneath the ice. There was no saving the dog.

I don't mention this to my father as we stand on the roof of his building.

He liked to scare us when we were kids, though that time I'm sure he didn't mean it. He'd lie around the house playing dead, wrestle with that dog and pretend it had bitten him, rushing into the kitchen to tend to the wound. My brother and I always followed, worried that it'd finally happened. That day, him submerged in the river, relying on the strength of his young sons, with only a loose grip on the ice and at the mercy of the current, my father was scared too.

"Pretty amazing," my father says after a while, "Isn't it?"

Besides the water, and beyond it, the city. The Kodak building with the burned out K, shining through the snow: odak. The restaurant that used to revolve while you were eating your meals. A noticeable part of the skyline. A place I've heard about, in grade school classes. Something that everyone mentions at least once when venturing into the city

for the first time. A place I've never been to. Not so far away
from the restaurant, the upper falls. A source of electric and
fishing and new cultural expansion with bars and art galleries
and restaurants too expensive to seem worth visiting. But the
view is nice. Sam Patch, jumping from those falls, not once
but twice. This another bit of grade school trivia, traded in
classrooms and on swing sets, and then one of those things
you think about when you're staring into the foam and at
those rocks waiting at the bottom. It's no wonder he died the
second time, his body lost to the river until the spring when
he came to the surface like a bobber out in the lake.

"We should get going," my father says, the three of us
standing shoulder to shoulder, snow piling on our hatless
heads. But none of us makes the first move.

IV. Down Twenty-Two Flights of Stairs We Go

Everywhere seems far away when the elevators are broken,
when you have to descend twenty-two flights. Especially in
this building. It is not the Hilton or the Sheraton, not the
new condominiums that have been built along the river and
in the arena district. My father tells us that were one of the
top two or three floors to catch fire, the fire department
would be unable to reach them with their trucks and normal
equipment. Everyone, most of them well into their sixties,
with walkers and wheelchairs, would be trapped. My father
jokes stopping to rest on eleven: "This is good practice," he
says, "just in case."

At the bottom of this building and a few blocks away in a
bar called Four Brothers, I will get to ask the questions that
another year has compelled me to ask. I will ask about my
father and his ability to descend the stairs in case of fire. I will
know, because with Dave there is no asking, only listening,
that no answer, or no real answer, is coming. My father will

probably die in this apartment, like Harold, and my brother will only continue to look more and more like my father and will one day forgive me for whatever it is he sometimes holds against me, for leaving this city and fleeing to college or maybe just—he thinks—for fleeing from him. My mother will never forgive my father but will one day admit that he wasn't so bad, not all the time, and she will admit that her boys are becoming more familiar to her each day as they look and act and become more like him. And this city, with its failing industries and minor league sports teams, and a brewery that has been closing for as long as I've been alive, all of this and then other things will happen and there are forces out there, and Dave reminds us of this much, that have conspired or been set in motion or which are out of our hands that make it so.

But Dave is not the only one trying to remind us. These reminders are everywhere, on the downtown billboards and on the signs in front of churches, in acts of crime and with the homeless man on Main who is shouting, "Hope is on the way." He says so but does not say when or how it is coming, but I suspect that this journey will lead us as far away from the answers as it might bring us to them, the way the river and the waterfall and the spectacle of a man like Sam Patch brought people to this city and kept them here. This myth is a way of understanding how my father lives his life, a room overlooking a city that on the coldest nights resembles a ghost town covered in snow, and the way it reminds me of an abandoned place picked over by the last few people to ever inhabit it.

V. Four Brothers

We sit in a booth, the three of us, sipping at pints of beer. None of us are talking but look instead into our drinks and gauge the atmosphere of the bar.

There are Christmas lights hung from the ceiling. On one end of the bar there are two Ukrainian men who are my age. They sit with a beautiful Ukrainian woman. Her hair is dark and wavy. Her legs are thin and long. She isn't the type of woman you expect in this kind of place. She is the only woman in the bar. On the other end of the bar there are three older black men and Uncle Dave. Dave is telling his favorite joke. A joke that begins: "Two prostitutes are walking down the street." The three of us, my father, brother, and I, are positioned at a booth in the middle. We're all in various forms of waiting.

It smells like cigarettes and spilled beer and fried food. John, the owner and bartender, goes back and forth from the kitchen, refilling drinks, frying food and cleaning. John is here to provide a venue. He does not come for Dave. He does not listen when Dave is talking. John comes and goes like a shadow; does not talk but knows when people need things. My father and brother go out to smoke a cigarette because it will be a while before it is our turn with Uncle Dave. I sit at the booth alone listening to Dave make jokes and tell stories to the men he sits with.

Dave leaves after a few minutes and joins my father and brother.

Inside the bar is quiet, and I feel uncomfortable without my family or Dave.

I drink beer fast and keep refilling my glass.

My brother comes back alone and sits with me.

He tells me my father and Dave are talking outside, talking about the war and about being fathers and about being drunk and falling on the ice. Dave told my father not to touch him when Dave slipped and my father reached to grab him. "If I'm going to fall, I'm going to fall," Dave said. And my father knew he meant no insult by it. This is the sort of thing Dave lives by.

When they return, my father and Dave, it is our turn. Dave buys us a pitcher by nodding at John in a certain kind of way, raising his Marine baseball cap and holding up two fingers. He turns to us, passing the pitcher from his bar stool to our booth. "In a town that dreams only of snow," Uncle Dave begins, "you spend a lot of time shoveling."

We laugh at this and drink to it in agreement.

"This storm is going to last until the New Year," Dave says.

"Just look at these boys of yours. Denis," he says "you done alright."

"Rass a Sass a Frass," Dave says. He takes his baseball cap from his head, revealing his dark thinning hair, and pushes his sunglasses down onto the bridge of his nose. He looks at me. His eyes are a deep dark brown. They remind me of the river. I sense the same sort of current in them. "It means, Hooo! Raaa!" Dave says, his glass in the air, a giant full-toothed smile on his face.

I know from years past, and just because you know when you hear Dave say it, what he means.

There is no talking for some time. We sit, the sound of John moving around, the buzzing of a space heater in the background. The television is turned to R News, which is a station that covers news in Rochester twenty-four hours a day. The reports are filled with statistics and there are charts and diagrams and pictures of plows and cars stuck in the snow and of kids building snowmen or skating on the canal.

Dave has a lot to say this year and we listen closely.

Still, none of us leave with a fortune. Or it is not the kind one would expect.

We sit there for hours, Dave moving from us to the men at the other end of the bar sitting with the beautiful Ukrainian woman. This is our fortune, all of it. The people who are there when you walk in and the charts and graphs on the television. The Christmas lights, some of which have burned out, and the three of us, father and sons, sitting here together for another year. That it is snowing and that we each have one pitcher of beer and that my brother and I will watch our father walk slowly, with a slight limp, back into his apartment complex where he will steadily climb those twenty-two flights.

I will stay in Ohio for five years, am still there, and when I drive home I feel like I am headed in the direction I was meant to move, east. It will always be my bearing. Not west to the new cities and prairies, not north or south to the poles. But east, home. I think about my father and wonder what the world will do with him. The markers pile up, each one drawing me in and propelling me forward: Cleveland, Erie, the rest stop at Angolo, Buffalo. Then the tollbooths and that last stretch of land, where the sky is gray, a kind of gloom that those who are not from here never grow accustomed to. And finally, the skyline: the smoke stacks of Kodak, the three giant tanks of beer in front of the Genesee Brewery, the smell of trash plates, the smell of river water, the High Falls, the Low Falls, the Eastman house, Lake Ave., Park Ave, and lastly my father's building towering toward the sky, and him in it, taking those stairs one at a time.

A FINAL SECRET BETWEEN THEM

Harold Lundy was dead and we were at his funeral. My father, brother, and I were all wearing wrinkled dress shirts and dirty sneakers. We stood by awkwardly; our bodies slumped at the shoulders, our hands crossed in front of us, our heads bent, staring into the dirt. Harold was my father's best friend. Other than us, there were three workers from the complex Harold was staying in and the nurse that took care of him while he was dying of cancer. There were three Marines dressed in their uniforms and shiny shoes, holding the American flag.

I felt out of place.

None of us belonged except for my father, with his dingy work pants and disheveled shirt. My father was the only one there who wasn't required to be. The American flag looked stiff and cheap. I couldn't get over how itchy it looked, how hard it was for the soldiers to fold it into a triangle. We'd been to another funeral a few weeks before, for our friend's father, and they gave him a twenty-one-gun salute. His flag was silky and so colorful I thought the color was going to run right off into his wife's hands when they handed it to her. There were hundreds of mourners there.

Harold had my father.

Afterwards, standing with the nurse, my father kept telling stories about Harold. He talked about Harold being a Korean War Vet. He bragged about how smart his friend had been, how generous and caring. Harold was the reason my father got into photography, my father said. And he talked about how Harold, in his handwritten will, had left my father everything in his one bedroom apartment, all the old books and faded clothing, and the gadgets, TV's and stereos that my father and Harold worked on in their spare time.

Shortly after that we went back to Harold's and we looted his place. I took a few paintings and books, two stools and a jacket. My brother took a set of speakers. We joked about taking the oxygen tanks yet to be removed by the hospice people. We fought through the smell of urine hovering over Harold's bed, and my brother and I listened close as my father told us those stories about Harold again. My father was a Vietnam War veteran. His best friend was dead. I feared his funeral might someday look like Harold's had.

My father touched everything in the apartment, offering it to us. But in front of his sons he took nothing. He kept moving back and forth between the bedroom and the kitchen making sure we were looking at things and building small piles. My father went back on his own. I liked to think of it as a final secret between them, my father and his best friend. My father took the things that were important to Harold. I saw them, days later, in his apartment: a painting of a Vietnam War Vet Harold had done, the books on radio repair and electronics, sweaters and shirts and jackets that barely fit him. I imagined him alone in that apartment that smelled like his friend, and I could hear my father repeating the words he'd said to us, "Take anything you want, take everything you can."

A LETTER TO MY FATHER, FROM OHIO

Dec. 1st, 2007

Dad,

I wanted to write and thank you for your letters and photographs. They have had a way of comforting me while I'm in Ohio. All of them bring me back to the city, carry me back to places I might otherwise forget, that I am afraid to let slip away. I really like to think of my writing and your photography as a way we preserve those things we love most, even if what we love most is not always there on the surface of things.

I especially liked this last series of winter shots. Winter is different in Columbus. It snows less but it gets bitter and the wind has a way of cutting right through everything, coats, windows, even, it seems, the walls. I turn the thermostat to eighty and even then the cold finds a way in. It makes me miss the snow, makes me miss the feeling that it should be cold and that it is kind of earned. There is something magical about snow here though, like the whole city shuts down for it, like it is some kind of holiday. Around the university kids use it to make lawn furniture and something about that makes me feel less alone.

When it snows here I think of you. I think of that old truck you had and how you'd take Jeff and me out to shovel driveways and how you made fliers for us, "Mutt and Jeff's Shoveling Inc.," how you thought it was so funny calling me Mutt. When I am alone in my apartment I think of that kind of stuff, think about what you said, how we are living similar lives. I really wish you could see it here. I think you'd like it. There is a cemetery at the end of my street. I go there sometimes and walk and smoke and think about you and your camera. I wonder where you are taking shots now and who you are meeting. I wish I could venture out into the world the way you do, meet people, and kind of dive into their lives.

Also, I wanted to tell you that you should let go of the past, just a little bit. That is what I have been doing in Ohio, trying to forgive myself for all the missteps, all the things I thought I controlled that maybe I didn't. You are a good father. I think about how you taught us everything, all the things a dad should teach their boys, obvious things like sports, but other things too, how to look at the world, how to ingest it. I think your photographs really made me see that for the first time. How you shaped us, me and Jeff, how much you really loved us. I'm sorry it took me so long to see it. I'm sorry I had to move away to finally understand. This, I suppose, is part of being human, learning from our losses how better to appreciate what is left in their wake.

Some day I am going to buy a disposable camera and take shots of my apartment for you and then I will take a bunch as I walk around the city. I know your van will never make it here. I understand too why you don't want to leave. I don't blame you. I know you'd come if you could.

Mutt

OBITS FOR PONY

Pony, also known as Burbs. Found in the lake, floating in his favorite t-shirt.

Pony, who was convinced he could invent a car that ran on water, left all his favorite cassettes with Evan Goldsmith the night he jumped, a final gift for that girl we were all in love with, who couldn't bring herself to love a one of us.

Pony, survived by a brother and a mother and even a stepfather who none of us liked but who seemed to, again and again, be there for his mother.

Pony, another twenty-year-old nobody, swallowed by sections a, b, and c of the newspaper and by sports on the local News.

Pony, who claimed he'd journeyed here from a planet named K-pax, while we were high and watching the movie by the same name.

Pony, who never told a lie.

Pony, whose cassette collection was something to marvel at, was something I would have traded my left leg for, who had his own kind of taste and style.

Pony, who cut through the water like a gull diving in for fish.

Pony, who jumped because he was bored, or it was hot and he figured he'd swim.

Pony, who had motive like any one of us.

Pony, who got his nickname without any of us reading that book, whose nickname is not stolen from it and who refused to watch the movie when he heard about it.

Pony, who kept two quarters stuffed in his socks in case his car broke down on drug runs.

Pony, who refused to use his quarters and called collect.

Pony, who rubbed those quarters together when we were sitting on the walking bridge, smoking, or drinking, or killing time. "They smell like my feet," he'd say.

Pony, caught in the current.

Pony, cashed in with his quarters.

Pony, calling collect, again.

Pony, the first but not last in a long line of early deaths, lives given over to the water, ghosts to haunt me.

Pony, a wrong number dialed.

Pony, a walking, talking, cartoon character.

Pony, in spray paint and carved in metal.

Pony, shoulder length hair and five o'clock shadow.

Pony, wrapped in seaweed like some mummy pulled from the bottom of the lake.

Pony, as an omen.

Pony, made into an After School Special.

Pony, swimming deep to touch the bottom.

Pony, my friend my reminder, remainder.

Pony, trapped in ice.

Pony, my obsession and obligation and outsider.

LETTER TO RALPH, FROM OHIO

March 1st, 2009

Ralph,

Just writing to say hello. Writing makes it feel like home, or writing to someone from home has a way of bringing me back. I don't know that I can describe it, how it feels to be so far from the people you love, even though they are only a long distance phone call away or six hours by car. Sometimes the flatness of Ohio seems to go on forever and when I drive west, headed out on a long drive, which I do sometimes just to listen to music or think or drown out the loneliness, the land is so beautiful like a giant green ocean and so lonely itself that I feel like I might never see anyone ever again.

The scary part is that, when I am in one of those moods and it is creeping up on dark and the right song is on I can imagine it and it doesn't seem so bad, that kind of solitude. When I am alone in my apartment in the mornings I get the same sensation. The complex is completely dead, all the sound of human life gone, the only thing left is the hum of the radiator or the buzz of the fridge.

Maybe this explains why I feel so different now when I am home. Why some of the guys seem put off by me or think I am strange. I can feel them looking at me and I can hear it when they ask about Ohio. They take my silence to mean I am judging them or that I feel like I am better than them now. But really I am trying to ingest all the noise, the sound of the jukebox and the jokes and the beer splashing on the counters. I am comforted by sound, find myself needing music or television at all times in order to simulate the sound of the places we knew when we were kids.

This place would be so much better with you guys here. But also I don't know that it would be what it has been for me. I feel parts of me changing, like the land does as you come up on Columbus from the east. How it flattens out only for those last few miles and there are vestiges of the hills and rivers from back home. It still feels like new skin, but some days it feels good, this solitude. Maybe Columbus made me finally fall in love with home, in love the way we should be with the places we come from, with the people who shaped us.

I sense that my time here is coming to an end. Ohio is feeling better to me, but it is better in a temporary way. I feel like I will leave a part of myself here. How could I not? It is where I finally grew up, or let go of the old ghosts, or maybe at least got comfortable with them being ghosts. I know that I've tested your friendship at every turn but that you're always there with a cold beer and sound advice.

I'll be home soon. One way or another.

Jon

SINKING IS THE ONLY WAY OUT

This story is an homage to failure: it is told underwater through snapshots or collage, in no particular order, without color. Is found at the bottom of a body of water, buried, stuck in the mud, unmoved by the current, like a bottle filled with letters that no one will ever read. It is hidden in the boiler room of a boat I once pretended to charter with my friends, is in those far away places I imagined taking that ship. Is a black eye, credential, sign of where we've been. Worn on the flesh like a map to sunken things, the ones we swore in blood never to reveal. Why keep secrets at all? Why hide things where they cannot be found? Why dig too deep? Why build ships made for sinking? Why this story, fragment, myth? Why all this crime—why does crime change or erase us? Erase an option, a way out? Why take pictures of this city, which doesn't know or care that we're in it? Why so much time spent thinking about it or the people you've lost in it—gone to the river or something far worse, gone like Kodak's factories and the flash of police lights and the ice from another winter? Gone the way of the brewery or Sam Patch. Gone like evaporating puddles of water, gone with the movement of trains along rails. Those people, friends and lovers and names on the five o'clock news, flashing like static on our TV screens. They are my father and his obsession with photographs and photography, his flashbulb firing off and out into the night. They are being carted across the River Styx by Phlegyas. They are not coming back. They are not rising with the ships or bringing buried treasure. They are other currents and misdirection. They are boys screaming at the moon where no one is sure what they're yelling about, screams that can be heard in every district in this city. Districts that have been meaning to yell all along. This is a reflex, a response, a way into the story, an end point like a building left to its burning. A timeline never getting longer. The rippling wake left behind from my father's outboard motor as I ferry out on his boat into the river, into the tall grass and places no one else but he and I know about. He tells me about fishermen and the way they learn the river, the way they know where and when to fish, and I imagine a similar but sunken place, where memory works the same way, where it is locked in a sunken boat, a secret, a buried treasue or one of those places only we know about, safe until there is almost no memory at all.

CAROUSEL

Jeff's never been on an airplane but he comes to the airport sometimes, every few weeks, just to watch planes take off and land and to sit around sipping coffee and thinking things through. This is a good place, he thinks, because people come and go, they are on the move, and he can figure something out about his own life and what sort of direction it needs. He's stuck in a low paying job with only his associate's degree, living in his mother's apartment. His only hope is to go back to school or to become a manager, and right now no one option seems better than the other. It's not that he's afraid to fly so much as he doesn't know where he would go or why he would go there.

He sits in a rocking chair, one of those touches the airport has added because of all the delays and cancelled flights, coffee in hand, feet propped on a railing, and watches outgoing planes. They move down the runway, lining up between his feet and taxiing away from him, and he decides on their destination, dreaming up passengers and elaborate affairs and business deals and maybe flirting with a stewardess like in a movie. In his mind the flight is all free drinks, four course meals, men in suits and women in dresses, all of them headed off to better places.

Jeff finishes off his coffee and decides to head to the baggage claim. Sometimes he stands there like a passenger just arriving and waits for a piece of luggage that is not coming. He rises from his rocking chair, throws his coffee in the trash so as to look sort of casual, and follows a large group of recent arrivals, all blurry-eyed and anxious to get their luggage. He spots a beautiful young woman, around his age he thinks, in her mid-twenties, and decides to follow her to the luggage carousel. She has one of those short punkie haircuts that are in right now and she has pale skin and freckles that make her look both beautiful and approachable, which he imagines is sort of a curse for a beautiful woman, seeming approachable that is. Jeff likes to talk to the passengers while he stands there, especially women, because they are always nice and they will ask questions about him and where he is from and why he has come to Rochester. This gives him the opportunity to create some other life or to be honest or just to talk to someone, which is often all he really needs.

As they approach the escalator Jeff decides to take the stairs. He doesn't want to get too close to the woman he's following, doesn't want to seem like a creepy stalker type guys, because he isn't. He takes the steps slowly, trying not to be one of those over-zealous travelers who arrives before the belt is even moving, as though getting there first will change the order the luggage spews out.

When they get to the carousel the belt is already moving, making that beeping sound so people will move back. Nothing is coming out yet and people set up camp, waiting for their luggage to come out so they can lunge for it and leave this place.

The pretty woman stands on the far end, where the baggage goes back in to complete another cycle. Jeff moves over toward her. He stands next to her and waits for the luggage, which has just now started coming out at the other end.

This is one of Jeff's common approaches. He stands next to a woman, waits for some piece of luggage, black, medium-sized, pretty mistakable for a million other pieces of luggage, and then he picks it up. Once he's got it in his hands he looks it over, sort of working his way toward the woman as if he is too preoccupied with making sure he owns this bag to be aware of space, and then he looks up at her saying, "Got the wrong one." From here he can talk about how all baggage looks alike or poke fun at himself for having such run-of-the-mill taste in suitcases. Most anything works because a woman waiting for her bag wants the waiting to run as smoothly as possible, even if that means entertaining a goofy guy for a few minutes.

In this case the woman says, "I know, for a second I thought it was mine." She goes on to talk about how she hates baggage claim and how they always lose her luggage or how it is always the last piece out. "Flying," she says, "just isn't all its cracked up to be."

Jeff lies and says, "I know what you mean." He introduces himself, uses his real name, which he figures offsets the lie about flying. "What are you in Rochester for?" he asks. He tries to listen, to pick up some detail he can work with, but he is worried about what he'll tell her if she asks. She says she's only here for a night, staying at the airport hotel because it is cheaper to do the connection the next day, in the morning, and that her final destination is Florida where her grandmother lives who she is going to visit for a whole month. Jeff doesn't know whether to lie or tell the truth when she asks, "What about you?"

A part of him wants to tell her that he is headed to Florida too, that he is going to visit his grandparents who are rich and have lived there forever, though these grandparents don't exist. Maybe he'll say that the two of them, Jeff and Nicole (he's picked up her name), should go out some night because it would be good to know someone who isn't a geriatric while he is there this summer. They could surf and walk along the beach and do all those other things young people might do while in Florida. But of course there is another part of him that wants to tell her the truth, to say that he doesn't know why he's here, to tell her that he is not a traveler but a local. He wants to ask her out for a drink, or ask her if she needs help with her bags. A part of him even wants to kiss her, to tell her that he is here to be loved by someone, someone who doesn't "have" to love him like his mother does, but wants to. Jeff wants to have that drink and then propose that they go to Las Vegas and get married and have a huge family, and though he doesn't make much money he'll promise to stop drinking, to mow the lawn, to hang the Christmas lights, to be there for the kids' baseball games and ballet recitals and graduations. Jeff will tell her, just as they lift off, "This is my first time flying," and as the plane levels off, he'll say that flying is indeed, "not all it's cracked up to be."

But now as she bends to retrieve her bag, "There it is," she says, Jeff stands on the edge of his fictional life and the truth, waiting for the next boarding call, for the next delay, for the luggage to make one more pass, some sign to help him find the way.

CHEYENNE II

That first night Ralph stood in the mud just looking at it. The tugboat had been stalled in the Genesee for ten years, sinking slowly. He'd parked on a side street along the river and walked through the weeds and mud and snow, like he had when he was a boy, to reach it. The boat had been abandoned when it caught fire and sat, mostly intact, alone near the banks. Ralph spent time on it with his friends when they were younger. He returned now, years after their visits had stopped, because the local newspaper reported that the boat was going to be towed after Independence Day. Sitting at the breakfast table, looking down at the article brought back memories, snapshots Ralph thought were lost. It was something he hadn't felt in some time.

He skipped his Men's League Hockey game to come see it, to not raise the suspicions of his fiancée, Janeen. He remembered the board his friends had hidden in the reeds and cattails, the one they'd used to get from the bank to the boat. He walked back toward the road, parting the cattails as he moved forward, searching for the board. Ralph remembered that in the winter it could get buried by the snow and remembered that they'd flagged the spot with a pair of his underwear, making him strip down after losing a coin toss, right there in the mud. Ralph stopped moving forward and made a circle, pulling his feet from the muddy snow, looking for any fragment of the flag. It'd be weather worn and faded by now, but he was sure it was still there. He pulled a small flashlight from his pocket. He moved forward. He made another circle.

In the plants surrounding the river any number of things could get caught. A few times Ralph thought he'd spotted their flag only to find an abandoned shirt or grocery bag. But finally, soaking and covered in mud, he found the board. Their flag was gone but he caught sight of the wood glistening in the beam of his flashlight. He lay down in the snow, exhausted from moving, from pulling his feet free of the muck. He looked up at the sky. The light from the city reflected off the clouds. He could hear the traffic from the bridge a mile down, listened to the sounds of the river and the cattails as they clicked together in the wind.

Every few nights after that first, Ralph returned to the boat, not wanting any of his old buddies or Janeen to know, because he couldn't imagine what they'd think. He was a teacher and a homeowner and worried about how it would look if they found him on the old boat, working on an engine that in all likelihood could not be fixed. What was he doing on it, anyway? Trying to relive another life? Trying to prepare it for escape? Trying to work away the last few months before he was married and tenured and perhaps, though he didn't think he felt this way, before he was trapped with that life?

Somehow he'd fallen into it, into teaching like his father had, into marriage like most men in their late twenties. He liked his life but he feared it, too. Lying in the cattails or standing in the water, working on that engine, made him feel like he was in control of things.

Sometimes he'd bring a six-pack and sit in the mud, staring up at the starless sky. As April came and May brought warm weather and wet nights, he could sit for hours, never even boarding the boat, just watching fireflies circle over the cattails, and on the edge of the river he'd see worms and snails and snakes come out after the rain, circling the puddles left behind. He felt guilty on those nights, when he wasn't preoccupying himself with fixing the boat. He felt like he was keeping a secret from his family and Janeen and his friends. And that guilt angered him. Though he'd never been one to keep secrets, had never stolen, cheated, committed any kind of crime, he felt he should be allowed one harmless secret and scolded himself for feeling guilty about it. Men have secrets, he told himself. And this harmless thing was his secret, even if he couldn't figure out why it was or what it was that he was hiding.

On the nights he did go aboard, he had to work up his courage to go down into the engine room. It was wet and cold and eerie down there. The boat, anyone could have told him, was beyond repair, but Ralph somehow believed, like boys taking apart broken things cast into the garbage, that some part of it could be resurrected. In the early months, when it was still cold, he'd warm himself in the Captain's Quarters, looking downriver towards the lake, expecting the Coast Guard at any minute. Sometimes, when it was dark and he could hear nothing moving, not boats or traffic on the Stuttson Street Bridge, he'd break off pieces of the sandwiches he'd brought, using them as bait and sit on the back of the boat fishing. He'd dragged a new board down because the old one was rotting through and he brought a fishing pole, a portable radio, beer, old manuals on engine repair, anything he thought to bring that might make the place feel more like it had when he was younger.

Ralph rigged a light to one of the walls of the engine room, running off an old car battery. When he was there, even with the light on and the radio playing, it felt and looked like the room had already given itself over to the river. The engine, which was not as rusted as he'd thought it might be, was the only thing there that reminded him of a boat.

He worked on the engine for hours, removing spark plugs, oiling the pistons, and as Independence Day grew closer, adding gas. It was a farce but he would play at it until his legs were numb with cold, until it crept into his sneakers, until he couldn't feel his toes anymore.

May came but the water was still icy, and though the nights were growing increasingly warmer, Ralph had to stop every hour to go topside and warm himself. More and more during those breaks, Ralph found himself cleaning out rooms or chipping away at loose paint or scraping at rust spots. He sat in one of the crewmen's rooms, papered with pictures from magazines, brought trinkets, hockey cards and clippings from *The Hockey News* in order to make the room feel like his own, even brought a pillow and blanket to lie in the bed and warm up. Sometimes he'd sit in the captain's quarters oiling the steering wheel or using cleaning supplies borrowed from home to polish the wood and clean off the windows. Ralph removed the mold and dust and brought a bottle of lacquer to paint over his name and the names of his friends, which they'd carved into the wood surrounding the steering wheel, forever freezing their names into the boat.

Sneaking out to the boat and sneaking back, Ralph would sometimes pretend to be hiding from someone, enemy troops or the police. It was a childish game and he laughed at himself, but he enjoyed it. He imagined his students, high school kids, doing the same sorts of things and it made him happy to think he still had that kind of imagination or ability left in him. To avoid attention Ralph tried not to park in the same place twice but this made it hard coming and going in the dark. Both ways he'd have to hop a fence and pass through someone's backyard. He never knew the lay of the yards, would trip over rocks or toys left out, and this had an element of risk to it that he liked. It was the first or last hurtle he faced before going in or making it out safe. Sometimes he'd lay low against the fence once he hopped it, pressing himself into the dirt and listening for people or animals moving. He thought about the lives on the other sides of those walls and in the woods and water around him. He would imagine eyes watching him and he wondered what they were thinking about him.

On the nights he was sure he'd been spotted he would stay frozen, pressed against those fences, waiting and listening and thinking about the world beneath the surface of the water. When everything went still and he was certain he was alone again, only then would he head home.

Ralph started, in the final days of June, bringing out charts and graphs. He believed somehow that he might still be able to make something of this, to get the boat moving and take it away across the lake and to another city or to Canada. It had become a kind of addiction. There was no telling now when the Coast Guard was coming and it was clear with each night he spent on the engine that he was wasting energy trying to fix it. He'd given up or at least given up on that possibility. He thought that by unmooring the tug and freeing it from the bank he might be able, with the giant prop, to maneuver the boat through the channel connecting the river and the lake.

More frequently, with school coming to a close and the summer settling in, Ralph would take Janeen down to Charlotte Beach, under the pretense of a walk on the pier or a trip for ice cream at Abbott's, but really he was scouting the area out, judging the width of the channel, the distance from the boat's home to the mouth of the river.

During the school hours he'd taken to making his kids do in-class writing assignments, looking up words from the dictionary and writing out the definitions, even though it was woodshop, while he worked on new benches, a new steering wheel, a second prop, just in case. His planning was meticulous. He took wire and car batteries and other items he needed from the auto shop and the electronics supply room. He took what he needed to make a simple wiring system from the steering wheel to the prop. He spent his nights at home in his basement with maps laid across his legs and piled on the floor. With different colored highlighters he'd drawn up possible destinations on Lake Ontario and he studied them, trying to memorize the names and locations. He thought about navigating across the Great Lakes and crossing into international waters. Once he was there the Coast Guard couldn't stop him. He'd be his very own island just floating in the middle of the lake.

As July approached, Ralph sat with weather reports from numerous satellite readouts and studied the weather, trying to decide on the right time and day. Night for sure, he thought. Getting out of the harbor would be harder then, more risk as visibility went, but there would be fewer boaters and no commercial vessels. He could get the electric working on the boat or at least the lights he'd need to get him out into the open water of the lake. He'd already had some success at getting the bunks lit and was sure within a day or two that he could get enough juice running to power all the lights on the boat. He wasn't counting on the engine anymore and that, in many ways, made planning easier.

When he wasn't planning out routes or going over the weather he was applying paint to any part of the boat he could reach. In its original colors, the hull was blue and the rest of it, with the exception of a few patches, white. Ralph had already, over the months, removed most of the rust and moss and applied primer, and now he was restoring the boat to its original state, adding in new patches of blue to flash it up. What was missing, and Ralph was unwilling to make a new one or go without it, was the original sign with the tug's name, Cheyenne II. He knew where it was, or where it should be, on their island strung between two tall willows. And Ralph believed, like he had with the board they'd hidden in the cattails, that it would still be there.

On the first of July he set out. The camp was a mile and a half from the boat, and it was rough moving in places. There were boulders and fallen trees and the mud to contend with. On top of that, there was the dark and Ralph's having not traveled the route in years. As boys they could do it by memory, could walk without flashlights and work with only the light coming from the end of their cigarettes, but now the path was overgrown and even if he could remember, it would take him a long time to get there. He thought about that, the overgrown path, and it was clear to him that when he and his friends had finally abandoned the island it might very well have been abandoned forever. Ralph assumed somehow that other boys would come upon these places, would lay claim to them. Perhaps, Ralph thought, this is what men require of the places they visit from their lives as boys, that they be alive.

The mud had mostly dried and the walk became easier. Ralph carried an old machete he had taken from his father's garage. They'd used it when they were kids to hack out the original path and his father had used it when they'd go camping to clear away space for their tents and gear. Now Ralph used it to cut through the cattails and drooping limbs with a steady rhythm, a kind of music. The sound of it, the blade cutting through the air and then catching something, cutting clean through, was good. Ralph felt like he was twelve years old again, pulling a cigarette to his lips with his free hand and clearing himself a fresh road. Sweat began to form on his forearms and neck. He could feel his chest moving with the effort of his heart and lungs, and the work was exhausting but satisfying in a way that teaching had not been and could not be for him.

When he reached the old clearing or what looked like the old clearing, Ralph sat down in exhaustion. The machete lay across his legs, hanging limply in his hand, and he pulled his shirt off, using it to wipe away the sweat from his face and arms. He looked around him, trying to estimate where the heart of it had been, where they had their camp. He stared up into the trees. He thought, momentarily, about Janeen and their house, his students and his parents—who lived four blocks away from him and Janeen—and then his friends who were still here, most of them, happy in this city and with the lives they were—all of them—still living together. It wasn't like some strange dream; none of them appeared there before him, not as themselves or as their former selves. Instead he just thought about them, thought about the way they might laugh or swear or say his name. "Ralphie. Ralphie Boy! Ralphie, you fucker!" Partly it made him want to turn back. And partly it made him want to go on even more.

He pushed himself up, leaving the tool on the ground along with his backpack and shirt. *There's no way that sign is still hanging*, he thought. They'd used a gnarled mass of rope to hang it. The rope hadn't been expensive or especially strong. *It's on the ground by now*, Ralph thought. He moved forward, his flashlight guiding him, and he kicked at piles of leaves and fallen limbs. He knew that the sign would be somewhere buried beneath the years of weather and vegetation.

Ralph moved forward, cutting through bushes, his arms and hands bleeding from small wounds, until he thought he'd spotted the willows. They were both overgrown, their branches hanging down like long fingers. They looked now, even more than they had when they were boys, like they had no business here and he knew instantly that this was the place. For a second he just stared at them. Then he noticed the sign, the edge of it sticking out from beneath the mud.

Maybe, Ralph thought, the only luck he was going to have was in finding things. He picked up the sign, walking back to his gear. He cleaned it off with his shirt, dipping it in river water. He strapped the sign onto his backpack and left his shirt there, lying in the mud. He walked out thinking about how lucky it'd been to find this place again. Ralph walked back towards the tug smoking cigarettes and trying to remember things about being a boy back when this place was still his. It was the first time, in all the months he'd been out there, that he considered the possibility that there was no fixing the Cheyenne II, that there was no way of fully bringing it back.

Ralph climbed aboard the boat, bringing with him his final set of supplies, some food and extra light bulbs and candles. It was the Fourth of July and he knew that soon the tugboat would be gone if he didn't unmoor it and attempt to flee. The engine was not running, but the lights were and the boat was freshly painted and everything, the graphs and charts, the maps and weather reports, had been posted in the Captain's Quarters, ready when Ralph might need them. He placed the supplies in their appropriate homes, save the six-pack he'd brought with him. He took a beer and sat behind the freshly polished steering wheel, starring out past the river and out toward the lake. It was eight-thirty and the sun had almost set and in an hour the city would be starting its firework show. They would shoot off over the lake from the end of that pier he and Janeen had walked all during June.

The first fireworks, amateur ones, shot off in the woods on the opposite bank and trickled down over the river. Ralph drank his beer and watched them for a while. He could hear a group of boys on the other side of the water laughing and yelling. He thought they might be shooting bottle rockets at one another, chasing each other through the woods on their way to the pier. He smiled, resting his free hand on the steering wheel and gently turning it from side to side, testing the tension and listening for the sound of the wires. He'd come to realize in the days since he'd retrieved the old sign that his plan was not going to work. He knew the patch sealing the crack in the engine room would come loose. It had only remained on this long because the boat was stuck, was neither taking on nor treading water. There was no real strain on it. But most anything, moving the boat, maneuvering through the channel—anything —might knock it loose or cause it to spring a leak that could not be fixed.

Now thinking about Janeen and his friends, his job and those kids on the other side of the water, Ralph realized how much of a fool he'd been. He could see now that it had been a dream, this fleeing. It was the kind of cowardly act other men took part in. They did it by having affairs or drinking too much. Some men even left, went on to new cities, met new women, started new lives and then ran again. Teachers, who were scared about teaching for the rest of their lives, quit or sabotaged themselves, swearing at kids or parents during parent-teacher conferences or stealing office supplies. And here he was, sitting in the Genesee River trying to rescue a boat he'd once dreamed of captaining as a kid, and he had seriously thought—for a few short months—that he could ride it off into the sunset like some cowboy in a movie. For the first time he knew that running wasn't him, wasn't the way he had lived his life and wasn't the way he wanted to live it.

On the nights when Ralph and his friends would go out to the boat, in the last few years before they gave up on the power of the river, he was the one who drove, stayed sober so they could drive instead of walk. He was the one making small repairs, fixing hinges and light bulbs. He was the type of boy who never told his buddies about the things he'd done with girls in his bunk when he promised those girls that he wouldn't. He was, like so many men, afraid of getting married, of being a teacher for the rest of his life, but he knew that it was this fear that had brought him back to the banks of the river and not any of the other things he may have wanted to believe.

He set down his beer. He removed the maps and weather forecasts one at a time, folding them neatly as he went. He walked down the hall to his bunk, taking the few trinkets he wanted, wrapping the blankets around everything. He walked out and threw them onto the bank and moved to the front of the boat, removing the ropes that kept it moored to the bank and letting them slide over the sides and into the water. The boat moved, rocking slightly toward the middle of the river and then rocking back again. Ralph stood there for a second thinking that the boat might come free, but it was lodged there. He turned around walking back past the captain's quarters and the bunks, headed toward the engine room. At the top of the staircase he flipped on the light and the radio. He walked down the stairs as he had on other nights and he moved into the water, bracing himself against the initial chill. He waited on the last step, the water at mid-calf, heard the fireworks from those boys on the other bank.

Ralph moved toward the engine, laughed at the new spark plugs, the polished bolts and cylinders. He hadn't made it run but he'd made it look like it might have once and he was, if only a little, proud of that. He moved past the engine and towards the back wall. The real Fourth of July show was starting now and Ralph thought about Janeen walking towards the fireworks with ice cream in her hand and it melting down the cone and her telling him, "Have some before it all melts away."

He kicked at the patch covering the old hole in the wall, knowing that once it came free the boat would take on water, become heavy on the one side, would roll out toward the middle of the river where it would, in all likelihood, sink. He kicked at it a few times. It didn't take much. When the patch came loose the water moved in slowly. It wasn't dramatic or high paced.

The hole was getting bigger now, the water angling to one side and wearing away at the burnt and rusted metal. Ralph dipped beneath the water. He pushed himself through, working his muscles against the incoming water and swimming out into the river. He watched as the boat tilted. It took a long time filling. It took even longer rolling. Ralph floated there for a time, moving his arms around, treading water. The sky over the lake was lit and the crowd down at the firework show was pleased. Then, finally, the boat flipped. The rusty and unpainted bottom had mud sliding off. The whole boat moved toward the center of the channel, slowly, and then began sinking.

Ralph floated there with his head resting on the water. Fireworks from the far bank hissed as they trickled down around him. The tugboat sank toward the bottom more slowly than he'd imagined it would. The air escaping from the boat and the fireworks firing off and those boys laughing and screaming at every explosion, it was a chorus, some sort of music for the sinking.

STRANGE CURRENTS

It's April, and the last hints of winter are just now lifting from Rochester. Dirty piles of snow still linger in the zoo parking lot, where it's collected from daily plowings. Spring won't really start in this part of New York for a few weeks, will be interrupted by more snow and lots of cold rain, will never seem to have arrived until the end of May when the snow has finally melted, though one suspects it still lies low to the ground deep in the woods where the sun hasn't reached it.

Pony's '91 Ford Tempo is parked in the woods behind the zoo. He and his brother, Aiden, and their friends are packed inside because Pony has the only working car, and it's everyone's way in or out of this place. Everyone hates his car, which does not have heat; the windows frost over and everyone is cold. Pony carries multiple ice scrapers, one for the rear and one for the front. The cloth lining for the roof is gone so people use the scrapers to write things in the foam ceiling. Aiden scraped the windows every few minutes because he is Pony's little brother and so Pony could see the road. Someone read one of the carvings out loud: "Pony loves dick!" The car is full with ten bodies, two in the trunk. "God, this car is a pile," someone says. People make fun of Pony's car because it is almost fifteen-years-old, because the back windows don't roll down, and it lacks heat. Sometimes, even in the coldest weather, they ride with the windows down so no scraping is required. They left the car and walked along the railroad tracks, snuck into the zoo through an old railway access that was never completely or properly sealed off.

Aiden licks his hand, his body sprawled out on the concrete, his flashlight—six feet in front of him—pointed towards his face. He's fallen; his hand is bleeding. His friends run by him, laughing. He can hear the sounds of the zoo, which they've broken into, can smell the elephants, whose cage he's fallen in front of. Aiden and his friends are here to jump into the polar bear exhibit, to swim in their large pool.

"Security Guard," someone yells.

And then, "Don't joke like that, dick."

Aiden picks himself off the pavement. He moves forward, reaches down for his flashlight and yells out, "Wait for me, you fuckers." He runs to catch up with them. This is a spring ritual, a sort of New Year's tradition, started by Pony. All ten of them are carrying backpacks filled with cigarettes and beer or bottles of liquor, but also they have each brought one item, a sort of offering to the polar bears.

Reaching into his backpack, Aiden checks to make sure his bottle of *Steel Reserve* hasn't broken. It is strange in the zoo at night, Aiden thinks, with the sounds of the animals pent up in their interior cages and off display, the pathways lit up by dim, humming streetlights. They've entered at the side of the zoo, next to the elephants and other safari animals and are headed for the back. There is no guard on full-time duty, just a few city cops who roll by every few hours and aimlessly make a once over. Everyone is loud, spread out, or stopped at different cages hoping to see an animal, to feed it some beer, or watch it do something it might not do during the official zoo showing.

"Check this out," Aiden hears someone say as he approaches the polar bear exhibit. He makes out, as he gets closer, Big Bear standing in front of the display and then, as he gets closer still, the only two girls who've come with them. He's showing them his bear tattoo, again.

"Looks just like him, don't it?" pointing toward the bear cage, though the bears are indoors, out of sight.

Bear thinks it impresses the girls. He shows every woman he meets. The girls smile when he says, "See, a bear, because I'm Big Bear," and he makes a growling noise. It's never really been cute, scares most women because of his height and weight, and just the way he does it with a kind of desperation. Aiden looks over at his brother, who stands picking the lock to the viewing area where the day crowd watches through the thick double-plated glass, beneath the water, the bears swimming.

"Come on you idiots," Pony shouts, hoping everyone will come.

The tattoo and Bear's showing it seem funny to Aiden, seems sort of appropriate in this place, if not for the reasons Bear hopes.

The last stragglers come running toward the exhibit, their breath blowing out in front of them. They move into the viewing area, loud and bumping into one another, and a few of them jump when they enter and see the huge stuffed polar bear looming in the dark observatory.

"Calm down," Pony says, "it's stuffed."

They all laugh and start opening their backpacks, fanning out around the oval room. The bear reminds Aiden of stories about little kids who've fallen into cages and been eaten, of the horrific ending which is the animals being put down. This in turn reminds him of Big Bear's father, who just died of a brain tumor, who Bear only knew for those last few weeks while he was dying. Aiden remembers the way Bear described it: "They put him down today," meaning they removed the equipment helping him breathe.

And Aiden thinks about his father's death. And then his mother, not dead but heartbroken, who looked so desperately alone until she found her new husband, who left Pony and Aiden to carry on the mourning.

Pony ushers everyone toward the glass. Aiden stands just behind them, the nine of them with their hands pressed to it, feeling it and looking out into the water, like a pack of school kids on a field trip. They are quiet for a second, and it makes the place, Aiden thinks, though he knows it's cheesy, magical. It doesn't last though. They get loud again, making jokes, fanning out; nothing can be too sacred. Aiden feels the urge to pee, is nervous about the guards and swimming in the bear cage. He pulls out his *Steel Reserve* and takes a few large gulps.

"We wait here," Pony says, "until we see the guards' flashlights and then hear them pass." He has laid down a blanket in the center of the room behind the benches people sit on to watch the bears. "Put what you're throwing in, here," he says pointing to the blanket.

"Look at this shit," Joey says from behind the merchandise counter, playing with the plastic bears and seals and penguins.

"Toss me some of those," Ralph says. A group of them, the girls and Bear and Ralph, sit on the floor making the animals talk as if they're in a porno.

They wait here killing time like this. Once they know they're safe, they'll take what they've brought and throw it in, two at a time, while the others watch from the safety of the glass room. They will race one another to retrieve what they've thrown in. The loser will be forced to stand watch or drink some of the Canadian Whiskey they've stolen from Bear's mother, which tastes like warm piss and fire and dick. Then later, after more rounds of racing, they'll all swim. And finally, just before morning, they'll leave their offerings in the pool to be found, hopefully by the bears and then the first visitors before they're removed from the tank for good.

Pony surveys what the rest of them have brought while they sit on the ground with their plastic zoo. "Who brought a dildo?" he says.

And then they all stop playing, come over to look, are laughing and making jokes about it.

"It's mine," Ralph's girlfriend, Janeen, says. "I'm retiring it because Ralph got me a new one." All the guys are laughing. They make jokes about Ralph being impotent, go back to playing with the stuff from the gift shop, drink from what they've brought. Ralph smacks people with the dildo, laughing the same feverish laugh every time.

Aiden sits on one of the benches looking into the tank. It's calming, looking into the dark water from the inside. Everything seems frozen in the motion of the water, its slight movement back and forth. Aiden can see the flashlights of the guards moving over the surface of the water from the platform above. He whispers for everyone to quiet down. For a second he thinks he sees their lights get caught in a strange current, like the water is trying to suck it in and keep it there, like the water is alive. Aiden feels like he is trapped in the underbelly of a giant fish, not a whale, but one of the river fish, a walleye or trout. Like one of the ones mounted on Ralph's uncle's wall. "The Marvelous Room of Murder," his aunt calls it, with all those fish and the heads of the different animals he's killed.

The flashlights pass, meaning the guards are headed toward the front of the zoo and back into the city. Everyone gets up, moves to the glass again. Ralph keeps slapping the dildo against it, saying, "Here fishy, fishy, fishy."

"Put that thing away," Janeen says.

Pony walks over to Janeen. "Since you've brought the most festive offering, why don't you pick the first two names from the hat?"

Janeen reaches into Pony's hat and grabs two pieces of cardboard, torn from a KFC box and stuck together with barbecue sauce, raises them into the air. "Looks like these two were destined for one another," she says.

Pony reaches out and takes them from her, looking at the names as he separates them. He smiles, looks over at Aiden. "You and me, little brother."

The brothers each retrieve their items from the blanket and show them to the room so everyone knows what they're fishing for. Pony has brought a Forzieri watch. "Made in Italy," he says, "Four-hundred and fifty dollars."

"Where'd you get that?" Bear asks.

"Stole it from Mark," and everyone knows he means his stepfather.

"Are you really going to throw that in?" Janeen asks.

"You bet your ass he is," Ralph replies, the dildo pointed at Janeen like a kid's toy.

Everyone laughs but Aiden.

"He won't miss it," Pony says when he notices the look on Aiden's face. "I've had it for a few weeks now."

Aiden resigns himself to it, isn't bothered by it the way his brother thinks, because Pony doesn't even live with them anymore, their mother and stepfather. But Aiden wonders if this isn't a sign, this thievery, about the future. He worries about his older brother, who lives in his car, who drinks too much and does things like this, this stolen watch, to get drugs or booze. Perhaps, even worse than a sign about the future, Aiden thinks, this is a sign about now.

The laughter dies down.

"Well, what'd you bring, you fuck?" Pony asks.

Aiden reaches down toward the blanket. There is no use worrying now, he tells himself. He stands up, a hockey puck in his hand, which he's written on in silver marker. He smiles.

"An old puck," someone says, "should be easy to find that in the dark."

Everyone laughs.

"Not just a puck," Aiden replies and proudly shows it off to the room. It reads "Ball Play" on one side, and "Is Overrated," on the other.

"Ain't that the God-honest truth?" Ralph says.

Aiden laughs.

"Well, let's have a race," Janeen says.

Aiden and Pony head out the door, round the corner, and make their way to the top of the viewing platform, fifteen feet above the water and even higher from their friends who are watching from inside. Pony puts one foot on the chain link fence and hops it with the other in one swift move. The bears are inside, but Aiden still feels a tinge of fear as his brother hops it and lands in the grass looking down into the water below.

"Let's go, pussy," Pony says, turning back to look at Aiden.

"Who's a pussy, you fag?" Aiden replies, hopping the fence in the same motion as his brother. He's barely on the ground when Pony grabs him, puts him in a headlock.

"Who you calling a fag?" Pony says.

They wrestle there for a minute, their feet on the edge. Pony goes to his knees trying to drag Aiden down into the grass. Aiden drops the puck, can see it just as it breaks over the edge, before it disappears and then splashes below.

"Let go, dick," Aiden says.

Aiden braces himself against the fence, trying to keep Pony from tossing him in or dragging him down. Aiden wonders if the guys can see them from below, the two of them wrestling.

He swipes at Pony's hands, knocking the watch out and sending it into the pool below.

"Shit," Pony says, "I wasn't going to toss it." He laughs.

Aiden leans away from the fence, pulling at the ass of Pony's jeans, and lifts him—Pony, who's always been the runt despite the two-year difference—onto his shoulder. Aiden thinks about his mother, about Pony, about himself, and tries to picture them with their real father but cannot.

"I'm still your big brother," Pony says, giggling and flailing his arms like a kid being dragged around by a parent.

"Whatever," Aiden says. And he steps to the edge, no longer resisting their movement towards the water. They are, in this instant, in this sort of awkward embrace, frozen. Then fall. A flash. A tangle of limbs, fusing. The flashlights of their friends below, beaming through the glass. The sound of the bears growing louder as they dive. The air swirling through their shirts and hair. Above them the sky turns and turns away, falling and falling and falling.

LETTERS TO PONY'S MOTHER

Dear Ms. Burkard ,

Forgive that I am writing to you on behalf of the Rochester Police Department to express my condolences.

Forgive that my words are of little comfort. I wanted to let you know we are doing our best to solve this and do so with you and your loss in the back of our minds. If there is anything I can do, personally, to help you during this time of mourning, please feel free to contact me.

Forgive me your loss, though I cannot take it back.

Forgive this city, which is incapable of apologizing.

Forgive the delay in regards to my letter. It was my intention to write you immediately.

Lord knows I've written too many of these letters in my tenure. Your son is the third pulled from the river this year and it's not even the end of August. I wonder often about the river, about those lost to it.

Forgive my discomfort.

Forgive my not knowing what to write.

Forgive this: my wife says I should just apologize for your loss, that there is nothing I can do to console you or set things right.

Forgive this: my wife says this sort of rambling is a sign of some deeper wound that I've yet to resolve.

Forgive our inability to effectively stop this.

Forgive all the arguments you cannot finish or the history you will not write.

Forgive the five o'clock news, which will seem like a reminder, and then daytime TV and newspapers and all other forms of mass media, which seem like an organized advertisement aimed at your grief.

Forgive those who know you and can't stop trying all sorts of things—vacations and other Hollywood remedies—none of which seem appropriate even to them.

Forgive the feeling to give yourself over to a, b, c...

Forgive the way you are coming to understand me, this unacceptable attempt to say something, to share grief.

Forgive that I mentioned my own grief.

Forgive, because it is unfair—perhaps—my overwhelming need to share something.

Forgive the forces that act on any set of circumstances, fate, for example, or luck. They cannot be held accountable.

Forgive the gods.

Forgive what has come to pass.

Forgive the way we all end up. Though finally it was too soon, perhaps. Though there is no way of knowing or taking it back.

Patrolmen Raymond Tantillo

GLOSS

Ruben stands outside the Rochester Port Authority smoking another Newport and waiting for his sister. He's halfway through his fifth cigarette, killing time before this yearly ritual, this meeting, and this meal that he is about to have with his sister, Kathy, who he only sees here, always in June or July. Other than this they only exchange phone calls on major holidays, Kathy sending gifts to his kids and Ruben for Christmas and birthdays. Which is why they meet here once a year to catch up, to talk about their families and lives and always about the past. And it is this, the past, that makes them avoid one another, because it is about their mother who was murdered so many years ago by Rochester's famous serial killer, Arthur Shawcross, and how their eyes and hair and skin remind one another of their mother and the wound that her death has left.

Ruben is early, scouting it out, thinking about skipping this year and just telling Kathy something came up with one of the kids. Inside the restaurant, called Cheeseburger, Cheeseburger, they have a promotion where if you can eat a one-pound burger, you get your picture taken and posted on the wall. Why would anyone do this? Ruben wonders. What is it about excess and photographs and being on the wall of a restaurant that is only frequented by kids on lazy summer days, because the ferry folded years ago and there is no real reason to be here, that seems appealing now, even to those kids? It seems like the sort of Hall of Fame one might want to avoid. But then Ruben thinks about when he was a kid. His mother took him here, one of those few times he remembers being alone with her, and he did it—ate the burger and had his picture taken. And now, inside this building, which is one of the reasons Ruben and his sister come here, there is a picture of him and his mother, the only one they know of because their father got rid of the rest. It is in a folder because the restaurant rotates the pictures out every six months, being that so many people have done it, and they keep them all in a photo album behind a counter, volumes of them. To their credit, Ruben thinks, Cheeseburger, Cheeseburger takes seriously their commitment to preservation.

Even if he leaves he knows Kathy will go in and sit with an overcooked burger and a Diet Coke and look at this old photo of her brother and their mother. She will call his phone and leave messages, which he will erase without listening to. But she won't hold it against him and understands the strength required to look again at their mother.

But he can't imagine her face anymore, his mother's, has this same problem every year. It is hard, he thinks, to remember with any kind of intimacy the face of someone he can't see every day, can't argue with or can't even call to check up on. He's forgotten the little boy sitting with her, his hands covered in grease and ketchup residue. He's forgotten who his favorite baseball team was, though he wears the hat. He's forgotten how his mother learned all the players' names, could talk to him about their batting averages and fielding stats. Inside, behind a glass case, in a cheap photo album, there is a picture that can remind him, if only for a few days, of her face and of his own when he was with her, of how life was before she was gone. The photo holds the ferry before it closed and became another symbol of this city's failing. It holds the event that cannot be stopped, that changes Ruben and his sister. It holds the last vestige of Kodak and film before everything went digital. It holds another year worth of things unsaid. It holds the river and all that has been swallowed by it. It holds those pictures of Ruben's mother that are gone now, on holidays, or just because there is value in preservation. It holds hope, the way the angle and the lighting frame her, and how the shadows and the people seem to touch her, and how the gloss of the photo makes her look, momentarily, alive.

STANDARDS OF MEASUREMENT

1.
Every single sunny day we skated, the neighborhood boys, at the end of my street. We played hockey until the sun went down. We skinned our knees. We bloodied our lips. We fought one another as cars rolled by, as neighbors sat grilling dinners, until the darkness forced us in.

2.
Johann Wolfgang von Goethe wrote, "Everyone believes in his youth that the world really began with him, and that all merely exists for his sake." We knew this in our bones when we skated in for game-winning goals, when we thrust our hands toward the sky to celebrate. Not even rain could stop us, though our rollerblades slid uncontrollably over the pavement. Every one of us swore at the cars coming down our street.

3.
We never carried our fears with us. Not when we were crashing to the pavement without helmets or when we were

knocking each other's teeth out. Everything we conquered, every tooth we lost became story, became our boyish way of lasting forever.

4.

One at a time, we took up cigarettes. All at once we got girlfriends. We were trying not to be boys anymore, all of us with our fables about women and sex. My friend Aiden claimed, "They call me the Captain when I tap that shit." On the rare days we still skated, between smoke breaks and arguments, I saw that none of us knew much about anything. Hockey in the street might have been it.

5.

Walking around late at night with six-packs in our backpacks and cigars dangling from our mouths, we'd find ourselves running from what we thought were police. It was Aiden who said, after four hours of hockey and a six-pack of Red Dog, "Dude. It's the cops. The car has two headlights."

We ran.

We ran because we couldn't stop our sides from aching with laughter. We ran because he had. And then later, when we left Aiden at his house, he handed Ralph and me a coat hanger, saying, "Carry this just in case."

I liked to think we were brave, but like all boys we secretly knew our limits and rarely shared them outside our circle. I tossed the coat hanger at a car when we were a block away and Ralph and I ran until our lungs felt like hot air balloons. We splashed beer all over ourselves on the way home. We knocked things over and sang and pissed on random things. Shopping carts and stop signs and people's front yards. We pissed rivers.

I didn't know much then, but I knew this: "Two headlights. It's a cop!"

6.

When our buddy Joe's father, Butch, died, every one of us showed up for his funeral. Even the guys we hadn't seen in years. In the year of our seventh-grade summer, Butch coached our hockey team and came every day to watch us as we practiced in the street. Huddled in hallways at the wake, we could be heard telling bad jokes Butch had told us during practice. One time he literally grabbed a clump of freshly cut grass and pretended to smoke it, lighting it on fire and saying: "Ya like smoking grass, do ya?" We all signed the hockey stick they put in his casket and bowed our heads when his grandson sang. Most of us had visited him in the months he stayed at home dying of cancer without health insurance, but we hadn't come together like this since middle school. None of us got close to the casket. None of us touched anything.

7.

"So what's next?" I asked. We'd been out all night. Joe drinking, all of us drinking, our collared shirts wrinkled and dirty and wanting off. The diner we'd landed at, open twenty-four hours, was packed at that hour from bars just closing. I remembered the nights we'd come here when we were younger, on dates, or after school dances.

"We gotta sell the house," Joe said. "My mom can't make the payments on it."

Later I heard a rumor that Butch had lost most of their money—not that there'd been much—gambling in Atlantic City, the place where he was "always winning."

"She's got some trailer lined up for us somewhere in the boonies."

We all lowered our heads and shut our mouths, sipped at coffees, and occasionally threw creamers at one another. I remembered the first time Butch had coached us, showing up and bringing Moutain Dew and Honey Buns. He'd hit it big that summer and bought all of us new jerseys and pants, bought me my first chest protector. I could see him now, faded work boots covered in pine and maple chips from his job removing trees. His front teeth were missing, and when he invited us over for team gatherings, we marveled at how he wolfed down chicken wings without them. He didn't know one thing about hockey, but he bought us new outdoor pucks and paid one of the neighborhood kids five dollars a day to chase the shots that missed the net.

All around us that night the diner buzzed, metal silverwear on plastic plates, coffee splashing into cups for refills, high school boys loudly jockeying for the attention of girls at another booth.

8.

Later that summer, after Butch's death, five of us worked a demolition job together. We swung hammers and dodged tiles as they splintered into jagged bullets and flew around the room. When the boss wasn't around, we'd go out back to smoke Marlboros and talk about cold beer and women and the Sabres' off-season trades.

"Can you believe these fucking rich people," I said. "Look at that floor we're ripping up. My mother would kill someone to have that floor."

"No shit, right," anyone would say, smoke floating from his lips.

9.

Our crew had a rhythm, the kind of rhythm you see in a man's walk, can feel when he shakes your hand. A rhythm working men carry around with them. The pulsating throb of the sledgehammer over and over again. Joe laughing madly as the tiles smashed. Music on the "heavy duty" boom box, designed to fall from any height. Breaks for cigarettes, water, lunch, sitting on the rich people's lawn and crushing it under our weight. You could time it, the arguments about who wasn't working hard that day, the conversations about how stupid this task or that task was. The giggling, the creaking of our shoulders as eight hours came to an end. And all that work was on our hands—bloody and bent and dust covered.

10.

A few days before we wrapped up work, a roofer fell off the house next door. When we arrived that morning, his crew was on the ground, all of them looking baffled with their hammers tucked into their holders like toy guns. We sat out front that morning throwing empty wrappers and leftover food at the neighborhood.

Our boss had told us he'd landed head first on the concrete porch, the same design as the one we were "not getting paid to sit on." And then we knew he had to be dead. There was no other way. The fall was at least twenty-five feet. The bricks jagged and solid and unforgiving. His head, someone speculated, had to look like meat from Taco Bell.

When breaks rolled around we said, "Fuck the boss," and instead of slinking out back, we went and smoked and ate on the front porch.

11.

The things we tore out of that house: tile, the wire netting under the tile, dry wall so much like snow when its powdery insides flew into the air. Molding, nails, cabinets, railings...I think if they'd let us, we'd have stripped it down to the frame.

Our favorite tools: the boom box, our lunch sacks, steel toe boots, the sledgehammer...pocket knives, caulk guns, cigarettes...the paint that got two of the guys so high the boss let them lie down for an hour while the rest of us worked.

12.

"Dude, you're bleeding everywhere," Ralph said.

My finger was oozing blood, a piece of mesh sticking right through it.

"Where are the band-aids?" someone yelled.

"No band-aids on a construction site," the boss replied. He grabbed my hand and looked at it. His hands felt crusty, carved. They were dark like they'd been dipped in motor oil and never washed, the dirt adding definition to the cracks in them.

"We just use duct tape," he said. He took the silver roll and ripped off a huge piece. Once around, twice, three times. "Tape the tip just so you don't get dust in there."

"Sweet!" I marveled at it. It seemed so simple to me, as if band-aids were now obsolete. All of my buddies laughed.

"Nice. It looks like you fingered a robot."

And the rest of our time there was like that. Cut. Duct tape. Bruised head from fallen board. Duct tape. Broke one of the hanger rods in the closet. Duct Tape.

13.

We learn slowly about numbers: sixteen inches on center, three feet to code, "Six feet down and you'll find heaven," our boss said.

14.

I'm sitting on a bar stool, years later, when these lines from Tony Hoagland run through my head: "We gaze into the night as if remembering the bright unbroken planet we once came from, to which we will never be permitted to return. We are amazed at how hurt we are." This is the language of lonely men. Those boys we were don't know this.

15.

We didn't realize, not on those summer days with packed lunches and bloody fingernails, between being boys and being men, that more than our bodies were being crippled. It's not until we're no longer working together, some of us on unemployment, me away at school that we can say: *we would give anything for what we had.*

16.

Butch's hands were one large callus. He walked dipped slightly forward like a blind man searching for home. He wore those wounds like armor, groaning when he moved from the couch, as he poured his coffee, when he put on his coat. All our lives we envied him. All our lives he told us, the guys on his hockey team, the guys who were working that construction job the summer he died, "Work only as much as you have to," he said. "Take care of your body." But we envied his sandpapered fingers. We desired his scars and stories. Our hands were soft and our bones were hard and we wanted so desperately to be men.

SOME RECORD OF WHAT WE'VE WEATHERED

Bear, don't think, run. Turn where you are and flee. Don't utter your mother's name, forget the name of this city. This place is a black hole sucking you in, keeping you here. You have no job and your unemployment checks are for $140 ($120 of which your mother keeps). You have a fiancée six hours away waiting for you to get up the courage to finally move away from your mother and this city, to marry her.

We sit in the old aqueduct, which is now just a fancy looking bridge, and cars are passing overhead and you are telling me how you're going in December, no matter what, no matter that you're twenty-five and you could leave now if you wanted, no matter that you may or may not have enough money for the bus ticket by then, may drink all of that money away with me, sipping slowly the thirty-pack of Genny we bought with the $20 that is your keep from this last unemployment check. We both know that I'll have to borrow my father's ailing mini-van, pack it with your one-thousand DVD's, fifty percent of which are horror films, and your garbage bag full of clothes, and your pair of dress shoes, which are your only shoes, and you wear them without socks because it is the summer and you say your feet are hot even though I tell you that it makes you stink.

We'll pack the van and pretend we're leaving this town like they would in one of your horror movies, zombies and all kinds of death and bad shit in our wake and in front of us. These monsters we run from are less scary than the reasons we're sitting, drinking a thirty-pack on a hot summer night in a place we hid out when we were kids, where bums wait out the winter, where our names and the names of presidents and war criminals are spray painted on the concrete walls. That fear, running from Frankenstein and Dracula, is adrenaline pumping, and women fawning and holy water and garlic and stakes through the heart. It's nothing like the anxiety we feel about you moving away and me going to college for my final year and then knowing, because I have a girlfriend there and maybe even a shitty, but sort of nice, teaching job lined up, that neither of us are coming back.

When you ask me if I'll come visit, I want to say no. I want to tell you that this is about disconnecting, for your good and mine too, but you look at me, your eyes welling up, and I can't say it because I won't mean it. I want to convince myself that I can shut this place out, hole up in a room with my lover and never come back, can forget the myths and stories, the hideouts and safe places we went to drink and terrorize one another. I want to tell you everything I know about marriage and love and family and being prepared for the worst, but I learned most of it from my parents, who are divorced. Though you'd only been with this woman for four weeks before you proposed, and she is your first girlfriend and you are her first boyfriend, and I know I should tell you to slow down, consider it, I don't because I am genuinely happy for you.

I know what you mean when you say you're not sure if you can handle taking care of this woman because none of us, our friends that is, the boys who love this city, will ever be prepared to love in that way. I understand how it hurts you when your mother says things about this woman, about how she is ruined, damaged goods, how this woman will never love you the way she does. It is more than your money your mother is after. It is your support. Your father is dead and she cannot raise your younger brother alone. You are her oldest. You have always been there, even in your own failed way, as a constant.

And there is, finally, distance to consider. The distance between you and your lover, the long distance phone calls we'll make in order to remain friends, which travel across wire and state lines and different nighttime and daytime rates. It is a map folded over until holes are worn in the creases. It is scotch tape on those torn up places and the feeling that the map has seen more of the world than we have. I make the occasional joke about your girlfriend and her buck teeth, and you call me "college boy," threatening to beat me up, and of course we forever talk about monster movies, as if we were boys again, making potions from salad dressing and shampoo and our mother's perfumes to ward them off, the monsters, the ghosts that have come to haunt us. And there we are hiding under the bed until our parents come home.

Knowing only they can rescue us.

LETTER FROM MY FATHER

Dec. 18th, 2007

Jonathan,

I wish I could make it to Ohio, but the odds aren't good. The van is slowly dying. I've been trying to use it less, but there is a good soup kitchen on the other side of the city and I've been going with my neighbor. I'm not really interested in her, or maybe she isn't interested in me, but either way she looks like your mother. We try to go weekdays for dinner. It helps me make ends meet.

But I would like to take a trip. I remember traveling when I was your age, the way the landscape changes, opens up somehow as you move west. I really loved that, the smell of the air and the way the land is so flat. Sometimes your mother and I would get in my 68 Impala and drive until we didn't know where we were. This was before we were married, back when I had just come home from the service. Her and your aunt let me use their names as tutors so I could get a little extra money from the VA. The only stipulation was that I had to treat your mother to a nice dinner every once and a while. Things were good back then.

The weather here is pretty nasty. Again, from this height everything looks pretty amazing. I bought some Christmas lights from the dollar store and strung them up around the window. At night I sit there, sipping on a beer, and watch the snow come down for hours. It is relentless. It piles up and just covers everything. But from here, before it makes it to the ground, the way it moves, the way the air sort of plays with it, it's pretty beautiful. Sometimes I fall asleep just sitting there, half a beer in my hand, my legs stretched out in front of me, the Christmas lights blinking off and on.

I guess you learn how to appreciate these things more when you're alone. I sent you a picture of the sunset from my apartment. I know you can't really get a true sense of it from the shot, but hopefully it gives you the idea. I sleep on the couch a lot, looking through photos, old albums from when you were kids, and the sun is my alarm clock. I like it this way. All the things I have left fit into this little room. It makes my life feel full, though I wish it was less ghost and more flesh, which is how it feels, the photos and trinkets, like they are more memory than material, like that 68 Impala and those road trips with your mother I guess.

Well kiddo, take it easy when you come home for the holiday. I assume we are doing the regular Christmas Eve and Christmas plans. I'll grab some booze. You guys bring the beer. Also, I got us a TV from the dollar general. It isn't anything special, but it works. Plus I've got some old tapes. Let me know if you need anything.

Dad

THIS PLACE IS LITERALLY NO PLACE

The city feels snowed in. The lead article in today's paper reads, "This Place is Literally No Place." It is about a giant hole in space, an area where there is nothing. The article reminds me of Rochester, reminds me of those nights, like the ones we've been having this December, when the streets are impassable with snow and the lake looks like the mouth of a monster, filled with ice and eating away at the banks, when this city appears swallowed by the weather.

We are going to my father's tonight, Ralph and Jeff and Big Bear and Aiden and I, because it is Christmas Eve and this is tradition. We are packed into Ralph's new SUV, a Chevy Blazer, with leather seats and fancy tinted windows. He got it at auction with a lemon lease on it, and though it is a six-year-old vehicle we think it is the best car we've ever ridden in, at least with any regularity. At my father's we will drink liquor and coffee and beer and we will talk politics and women. My father lives a few blocks from Avenue D, which is infamous for all kinds of things—crime and graffiti and violence—though we all think it's overblown. The city has a way of becoming myth.

My father seems comfortable in this apartment, twenty-one floors from the ground. From up here we can all look out on the city and make our own assessment. My friends come here because my father is a good storyteller, because he likes having us around, and because he tells a good joke. We come because in some ways we idolize him and in others we wonder if this isn't what our lives might some day look like.

There is snow in the air, like most nights in December, but the real storm isn't going to be here until tomorrow. You can taste it in between puffs of cigarettes while standing outside my father's apartment. This is a good sign as far as Christmas is concerned. We aren't big fans of snow, seeing that we get so much of it, but even we wish for a nice dusting on Christmas.

Once we've settled in my father tells us that we should let go of the ghosts that haunt us. Especially me. He says I should stop writing about Arthur Shawcross and Ruben and my dead friend Pony. He says it bothers him when I write about these things, that I am taking advantage of these incidents and the people involved in them. He also says I need to lighten up, that all of us need to lighten up. My father, who was a janitor, has lost his job or quit, it is unclear, but he has just enough money squirreled away to make it for a few years in this subsidized apartment and he says, "I intend to enjoy every minute of it." He also says, holding a bottle of beer in his hand, "You all need to cut back on the booze. You're running from something and using this crap," he raises the beer towards his lips, "to get away from it."

I laugh and say, "You don't seem to mind drinking it."

He looks mad. He does this a lot, tells us one thing and does another.

I am afraid to tell my father that I cannot let go of Pony or Ruben. I continually dream them, and I write about them so that they will not be forgotten but also because I feel that if I put them down on paper, preserve them, that they might finally leave me alone. I fear, though I'd never admit it, that my father is right about our drinking. We are all hiding from something. All of us live at home with our mothers, with the exception of Ralph whose parents are still together, and Ralph will buy his own house soon, move out of his parent's basement. But, even that, the prospect of his own life, scares Ralph as much as not knowing where we're headed scares the rest of us.

A few hours in and Big Bear is crying. This is common. He is six foot four, weighs two hundred fifty plus pounds. He is a giant, as his nickname would suggest. Despite his size and what we've come to call "retard strength," Bear is extremely sensitive. And with his hands, monstrous paws, that grab us when we make jokes about him, or when he is giving us a hug—as he often does—it's like some animal squeezing the life out of us. Most nights we rib him about the crying, which comes twelve or thirteen beers deep. We call him "pussy" or "fag," the types of names men use when they are acting like boys, when they are uncomfortable with the state of things. We get squeamish and act defensive around people's emotions, especially the emotions of other men.

What's brought us here, to the point where Big Bear is crying, is a conversation about class and race. The conversation has gotten heated. It has also gotten to the point where we may all be agreeing about it, about which of these issues is most pressing in this city, but we've lost sight of that and are raising our voices louder and louder, calling one another "fucker" and "asshole." We say things like "You're not listening, you prick," and other things we don't mean. But there is the booze and it is Christmas Eve, or actually—past midnight now—Christmas, and we are comfortable with one another, comfortable enough to have these sorts of fights.

Just beneath the shouting there is Bear, his hands over his face, large gulps of air sucking in and sucking out.

"You guys shouldn't be fighting like this," he says. "We're all family. You should love your family."

The crying is full on now. Saliva and tears and snot drip down onto his fake leather jacket, which reads "Beer Guy." His whole body convulses when he gets like this. If you haven't seen it before you might think he's going mad.

"Come on Bear," my father says, "don't get upset."

"Yeah bud, it's alright," Aiden says, trying to hand him another beer.

What's really got him is that his grandmother died a few nights ago. She died unexpectedly, sort of. That is, she was eighty, a long time smoker, had been living off Social Security and disability, but no one expected her—three days before Christmas—to not wake up. On the coattails of that there is his family's economic situation. They're on welfare. Between his grandmother's Social Security checks and the ones his mom gets, they were paying the mortgage and eating. Without his grandmother they won't be able to do one of those two things and though Bear—as well as the rest of us—doesn't know this yet, it means they're going to stop paying the mortgage, going to eat and live in that house for as long as they can until the bank forces them out.

We sit staring at my father's television, which is muted. Bear has gotten control of the noise but he is still crying and it is coming hard. The wind rattles the old window that looks out on the city. Bear's jacket is covered in tears. I grab paper towels trying to wipe him up. There is nothing that anyone can say or do to fix it. His grandmother is dead and we are here, like we always are, and we don't know what to say about his loss or about our own losses. Silence is how we tend to these wounds.

It is dark in my father's apartment, the only light comes from a string of Christmas lights strung around the bay window and the television, which flickers from commercial to commercial like a single eye blinking and staring in on us.

After Bear gets control of his crying, Aiden takes him downstairs for a cigarette and some fresh air. My father is holding a beer in one hand and nodding off in his chair. He is facing the window as if he is standing guard over the city. He snores occasionally and Ralph and Jeff and I laugh, making jokes about the old man not being able to hack it anymore.

When Bear and Aiden come back we pick up a bit and leave my father sleeping in his chair. I know I'll see him tomorrow when my brother and I meet him to go to a bar in his neighborhood, but I feel a bit guilty leaving him there, the light outside just now starting to match the glow of his television. We laugh and drunkenly crash into things as we exit the building.

I won't be here much longer. I live with my mother when I am home on breaks and for the summer, but I will go back to school before the New Year. I plan to spend more time with my father and my friends before I leave. I am on the verge of being out of this city forever and that scares me and I worry sometimes that there may be no way, if I am gone long enough, for me to come back.

Outside the sky seems lit by the city, the street lamps, the Kodak building, the Christmas tree in the center of town. Everything is illuminated like this city is some sort of landing zone, some sort of refuge from weather or emergency, though I can't imagine why anyone, on a night in December, would come here. Snow is coming down slowly, landing like a layer of dust, residue from a flashbulb, on top of the snow that has been here for a solid month. It actually looks and feels like Christmas. I imagine letters sent from children all over the city filled with wish lists and prayers and questions about elves and reindeer.

We pile into Ralph's Blazer. We're blasting Christmas music and singing along. Aiden is in front with Ralph. Bear is pressed between my brother and me. We have our arms around him, are encouraging him. "Come on, sing with us Bear," we say. None of us knows all of the words to any of the songs but we know the choruses. Ralph has rolled down the windows and we're screaming out the lyrics at the top of our lungs. "Jingle Bells," and "Silent Night," and "Joy to the World." We add in our own twists when we see fit, nothing clever, a "balls" substituting for bells, an "all is well 'cause we're drunk tonight," a joy to the "fucking" world just because it seems right in the cold air swirling through the car as we fly down city streets. It is 3:00 A.M. and it is snowing and we don't, not one of us, want to go home.

I think about our mothers, what they are doing. Sleeping, no doubt. I wonder if they are worried about their sons, if they imagine us doing the things we are doing. I think about my friend Ruben and his mother, murdered years ago. I think about my friend Pony, who is dead now, wonder what his mother is doing tonight without her oldest son. My own mother will be awake when my brother and I walk in around seven or eight. She will have coffee ready and she will be in her chair doing her crossword puzzles. The two-foot tall artificial tree I have put up for her in her apartment will blink one, two, three, one; one, two, three, one. My mother will smile at us and run her hands through our hair and she won't ask where we've been. She knows. In a few days my father will develop the two or three disposable cameras worth

of pictures he shot. He will give all of us a stack to remember
this Christmas Eve by. My mother can look through them, a
sort of index. She can reference them whenever she wants to
reach her sons or even, in a private, more lonely moment, her
ex-husband.

The streets are empty. We are the only vehicle out at 3:00
A.M. on Christmas Eve. We wish the city a Merry Christmas,
the music blasting, our heads outside the open windows.
"Merry fucking Christmas, Rochester," we yell out. And we
mean it. We have come to love this city as cold and lonely as
it may sometimes be.

We talk for a bit about going home. Ralph gets on the
highway and heads toward my mother's apartment.

Once we reach the parking lot, Ralph pulls into the bus
loop. He turns the music down and asks what we all want
to do. In the back seat Bear has just lit a cigarette and my
brother has just opened a beer and no one wants to admit
that we are, perhaps, a bit afraid of where the night will take
us. With the streets empty like this it feels like we own the
city, like the rest of its populace has disappeared, and we are
not ready to give that up yet.

I can smell burning wood coming from the fireplaces of
the houses next to the complex.

Ralph puts the truck in drive and fishtails out of the bus
loop. The windows are up now and we head back out into
the city. My brother passes a beer to Aiden and Big Bear and
me. We splash them all over ourselves and the car and start
singing "Have Yourself a Merry Little Christmas." Ralph
doesn't seem to mind, though he is the only sober one and
would normally object to our drinking in the car. He looks
out through the snow and drives us into the city, toward the
art gallery and the Xerox building. He seems like he knows
where we are going and in the midst of this, the music and
my friends and the smell of burning wood still lingering in

the car, I feel like we all have a temporary sense of direction.

We pass a pair of RPD cars parked at the Hess station where Browncroft turns into Atlantic. They don't seem to notice us.

Every yard is filled with some sort of lawn ornament. They get more and more gaudy as we get closer and closer to the city. I like that.

There is the possibility of us all making it out or maybe even staying and making something of that. There is my father who has spent his whole adult life here, who is passed out in a lawn chair right now, facing the city. He reminds us that there is nothing wrong with staying, that there is no need to start over again or run away, that there is no place, no matter how high off the ground, to go, where we will not—sooner or later—have to face ourselves.

We hurtle forward into the city. My father has his photos of the night, which we will see later. He has some from our arrival and some from the point where we were just getting drunk. There are shots of all of us together and solo shots. Mostly there is the window facing out onto the city and the river below and the ghosts of friends and acquaintances and maybe even Big Bear's grandmother. We are all facing the window in one picture or another, looking out as if there is someone on the other side looking back. I see things in the reflections, in the underdeveloped film, smoke or something floating around between the Christmas lights and our bodies and the flash of the camera. There is nothing there, no ghosts, it is a trick—exposure or lighting or angle. Maybe it has something to do with how high we are off the ground. I just know I can hear the river and smell the snow. I have given so much of myself to the friends who are gone, lost to the river, and I begin to wonder if I can ever let them go or if it isn't my fear of living without this loss that makes me write them over and over again.

In my apartment I have pictures of the other places my father has taken photographs. My friends and I playing hockey in the street, boys jumping from locks at the Erie Canal, churches, and abandoned parking lots, and other odd and somehow welcomingly lonely spots. I have history books about some of these places and have tried to put stories to them, to put some other kind of meaning to my father's photographs.

We end up at the canal, parked a mile from one of the old locks where in the summer boys come to jump into the muddy water. There are ghosts here too. Ghosts of the canal diggers and lock operators and boys who have died jumping.

We leave the car, carrying stray backpacks pulled from Ralph's SUV. We fill them with cans of beer. We also bring the hockey sticks that are in the back, stored for his Men's League games. We're not sure what we're doing here yet. The path down to the canal and the mile to the lock is unplowed and we'll have to walk through the fresh snow, but there is no conversation about whether to do it or not. We walk. We are like a troop of soldiers or refugees, backpacks and hockey sticks slung over our shoulders, beer in our hands. Ralph starts singing "Low bridge everybody down..." and I follow, "Low bridge we're coming to a town." It is an old canal song, one we learned in grade school, and though it is not a Christmas song we, all of us, start singing it like it is, marching in line, each man following the footprints in front of him, snow sticking to our heads.

Ten minutes later we reach the lock. We climb down the banks of the canal. The water level is down and this means that the canal is iced over or if it isn't we'll only be to our

waist in water so the risk of checking is minimal. We set our
things in the snow. We test the ice, which is strong.

"What now?" Aiden asks, throwing an empty beer can.

"Hockey. What else, you ass clown?" I say.

This summer the city will start tearing down old Kodak
buildings and they will cart out the rubble on old canal boats.
One faded technology will carry out another. The city is like
this, it has its own losses to mourn. Those canal songs we
learned in grade school, even those may some day, I fear, be
obsolete.

But now we slide around on the ice. We are trying to clear
the surface of snow so that we can play hockey with the sticks
we've brought and an empty can of beer. Ralph slides with his
arms outstretched, clearing the snow like some kind of human
Zamboni. The rest of us follow. We are all soaked, covered
with snow and smiling. When we have a decent square cleared
we take two backpacks and use them to make goal posts. We
throw Bear in goal and he slides around without a stick trying
to protect the goal and smoke a cigarette and balance his beer
all at the same time. My brother and I play against Ralph and
Aiden. We run around for an hour or more. We check one
another into the banks. We slide into the goal and pile on
one another. We even get heated about Bear not taking his
job seriously enough.

Soon we are out of breath. Our skin is red and our fingers
are waterlogged underneath our gloves. We climb the steel
sides of the lock, one by one. We know eventually we will
have to go home. But for now no one talks. The sky is turning
orange as the sun rises in front of us. We sit with our legs
dangling.

I don't know who it is, but someone starts singing that
canal song again. He sings it softly with the hesitation of a
boy who is unsure of his actions. But it doesn't take long to

catch on. We sit there singing, the five of us, with the last of what energy we have left.

Our heads twist upward toward the sky. The snow melts on our warm skin.

Nothing has changed or been solved. There is no resolution or intention of changing things and there aren't any coming. We are all right with this.

ACKNOWLEDGMENTS

Thank you to the editors of these magazines where pieces of this collection first appeared:

Admit2: "In a Town that Dreams Only of Snow"
The Disability Studies Quarterly: "The Ins and Outs of Science"
Drunken Boat: "The War at Home"
Flashquake: "Other Lives"
              "A Final Secret Between Them"
Glimmer Train: "This Form of Grieving"
Hobart: "Pulled From the River"
Hotel Amerika: "Undertow"
Monkeybicycle: "X-Ray"
Pindeldyboz: "Sum"
Redivider: "Standards of Measurement"
Smokelong: "The World Before This One"
Staccato: "Letter to Jeff, from Ohio"
Sweet: "Coroner's Report"
         "Letter's to Pony's Mother"

Swink: "Letter to Ralph, from Ohio"

Upstreet: "This Place is Literally No Place"

Waccamaw: "Some Record of What We've Weathered"

Wordriot: "Sinking is the Only Way Out"

"The Bright Night Effect"

You Must be This Tall to Ride: "Strange Currents"

APPENDIX

A Guide to the Text and Secondary Sources

This Form of Grieving

Pictures of the tugboat, Laundromat, and other miscellaneous
   photographs can be seen at:
      www.pulledfromtheriver.com
For Klassy Cat Information such as:
   Business Hours
   Directions
   Or a cumulative index of current "talent"
      Visit: www.klassy-cat.com
   Field of scholarly interest: Photography
   Secondary interests: Story, Family, Consumption

Pulled From the River

- The opening line: *When I tell you this story, remember it may change,*
   is borrowed from a Sherman Alexie story: *Captivity*

- The line: *Every passion borders on chaos, that of the collector on the chaos of memory*, is borrowed from Walter Benjamin.

  Other Important Things to Consider:
  - Don't believe everything you read.
  - **Storytelling** is the ancient art of conveying events in words, images, and sounds often by improvisation or embellishment. Stories or narratives have been shared in every culture and in every land as a means of entertainment, education, preservation of culture and in order to instill moral values.

The Bright Night Effect

- *All at once the world feels beautiful, more than I can say,* is a line donated by the poet Ruth Awad.

The World Before This One

- To view a documentary about The Genesee River Killer visit: http://www.hulu.com/watch/100061/biography-arthur-shawcross

In a Town that Dreams Only of Snow

- The title is pretty much stolen from a Paul Guest poem: "Illustrations"
- Four Brothers, as one might expect, does not have a web page.
- If you are from Rochester and "of age" you can get information about one of these lovely apartments by visiting: http://www.rochestermanagement.com/

Standards of Measurement

The line, *We gaze into the night as if remembering the bright unbroken planet we once came from, to which we will never be permitted to return. We are amazed at how hurt we are,"* comes from Tony Hoagland's poem, *Jet*.

The line, *we would give anything for what we have,* comes from Tony Hoagland's poem, *Jet*.

If you are interested in remolding, demolishing, or adding on to your current home feel free to contact C &R Construction. Ask for Ralph.

Letters

I would like to thank K.C. Wolfe, who wrote a series of letters for the manuscript he is working on and was kind enough to share them with me. The beauty of those letters inspired my work and gave me the idea to add something like them to this manuscript.

This Place is Literally No Place

Thanks go to my father for sending me a newspaper clipping entitled: "This Place is Literally No Place."

Thank You

a) To my parents. You have always supported me. There is, of course, the literal my not being here without you. But then, there is my not being here without you.

b) Stephen Kuusito who took me under his wing when I most desperately needed a friend. I am sorry I was such a child at times. Your ability to listen, your faith in my work, and your enthusiasm for sports and beer got me through all of it. You always left me wanting to write.

c) Ira Sukrungruang who made me want to write and stuck with me through all the false starts, failed love affairs, and childish antics. Without you there is no book to speak of. I can't begin to tell you how much your friendship means to me.

d) Katie Riegiel, whose patience with my inability to fully or even partially learn anything about English grammar has made me, for a long time running, appear smarter than I truly am. You have always been, more than my teacher, a dear friend.

e) Lee Martin whose encouragement, looks of disappointment, and ability to teach changed my writing and me in very important ways. Your continued friendship and belief in me kept me sending the manuscript out and trusting that someday it would be a book.

f) Ruth Awad, who pulled me out of the dark, worked to make me a better writer, and read almost every draft. Your fingerprints are all over this book.

g) To these people, who I can not thank enough for being there: Jeff, Ralphie, Big Bear, Smitty, Joey, Porras, Mike, Lesh, Steven Daniel Ward, Kim Possible, Jackie, Doc Kyle, Janeen, Lindsay Pizzo, Uncle Cas, Mr. and Mrs. P, Amy, Jason, K.C. Wolfe, Sarah F., Leigh Wilson, and Dr. Frank Byrne.

h) To Greg and Josh who were patient with all my demands, changes, additions, and other bullshit. You guys made the best website ever. No doubt. Thanks for everything.

i) To the people who work tirelessly for Black Lawrence, especially Diane, who took a risk on my writing, provided it with a home, and was always patient with my emails, goofy questions, and over eagerness. I am proud to be a part of your press.

j) Finally, thank you to all of my teachers at SUNY Oswego and The Ohio State University. You shaped me, held me accountable, allowed me— for a time— to be a child, and finally made me grow up.

Appendix:
For cut scenes, additions, character profiles, audio, and other parts of the text generally missing from the book itself, visit the appendix at:

WWW.PULLEDFROMTHERIVER.COM

JON CHOPAN was born and raised in Rochester, New York. He received his MA in history from SUNY Oswego and his MFA in creative nonfiction from The Ohio State University. His writing has appeared in journals such as *Glimmer Train*, *Hotel Amerika*, and *Post Road*. Currently, Jon lives in Columbus, OH in a shoebox.

For more on this author visit:
www.jonchopan.com